ONE

HOGAN BROTHER'S SERIES
BOOK ONE

CHANCE

USA TODAY BESTSELLING AUTHOR

K.L. DONN

ONE CHANCE

HOGAN BROTHER'S BOOK ONE

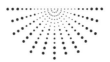

K.L. DONN

Credits:

Edited by – KA Matthews

Cover Design & Formatting – Sensual Graphic Designs

❀ Created with Vellum

"Stupid."

One word that could ruin a person.
One word that can change a life.
One word that can destroy a mind.

Soph

Sophia Bennett heard it all her life. Smart, sweet,
and shy, she hesitated to voice her ideas and
opinions in fear of hearing that dreaded word,
"Don't be stupid, Sophia."
She became introverted, quiet. Talking to people
became a struggle she fought to control. She turned
into a woman she never thought she'd be.

Seen but never heard.

Appearance became everything.

Nox

Rough around the edges Lennox Hogan is knee dip in shit – literally. Building a garden for his mother with his younger brothers, when the most beautiful creature he's ever seen stops by to visit their mother for their weekly book chat.

A fake smile and sad eyes draw him in.

Her intoxicating innocence has him obsessed with the need to know everything about her.

An unknown threat has them questioning everything about her life.

Lennox soon makes it his mission to convince her to give him One Chance, but will she after her world crumbles before her?

For my readers.
Thank you for sticking with me.

PROLOGUE

NEVER LOVE ANYBODY WHO
TREATS YOU LIKE YOU'RE ORDINARY.

"Sophia!" She had heard her mother before she saw her. A quick look around assured Sophia Bennett that her room was tidy, the bed was made, and she hadn't recalled leaving anything out when she'd arrived home from school.

Footsteps in the hall announced her mother's arrival. Standing quickly—shoulders back, and her back straight—she waited for the berating to begin.

"Did you hear me?" her mother, Rebecca—never Becky or Becca—Bennett demanded as she flung the door open.

"Yes, Ma'am," was the only reply she knew would be acceptable.

"Well?" The tapping of her foot on the hardwood floor could be heard. "Why didn't you answer me?"

Sophia's brain blanked…

One would think they could just say, *I heard you coming*, but she knew that wasn't an appropriate answer for her mother.

So she stood there…

No words forthcoming, no immediate answer could be given.

"You can't be that ignorant, Sophia." The censure in her voice made Soph feel lower than dirt.

"I'm sorry, Mother," she whispered.

"I don't want your apologies; I want to be sure you're going to be ready for tonight. By your appearance now, I can tell that's obviously a no." Disgust crawled across her mother's botoxed face.

"I will be," she promised. It was the only time she would get to see her great Aunt Millie. She was the sweetest old woman Sophia had ever known. Always had a funny story to tell and little candies in her over-sized purse for her. It was but once a year now that she actually got to see her.

Aunt Millie had fallen ill two years ago, and travel was hard on her aging body, so Sophia's mother didn't let her come across the country from New Jersey to visit them.

Her father was head of security for one of the largest criminal law firms on the west coast. The attorneys he kept safe were made targets by their clients, so he assured all meetings went smoothly.

Last summer, one of the lawyers lost a case for some drug dealer—she didn't recall the charges—but the defendant's gang retaliated and wound up paralyzing the man. It brought home how dangerous her father's job was.

He was a good man and treated Sophia like a princess, as if she were his whole world. She sometimes wondered if that was why her mother hated her so much. They didn't sleep in the same room anymore, and she couldn't remember the last time they did. And when he *was* home, they barely said two words to each other.

Snapping fingers in her face ended her internal analyzation of why she was so hated. "Earth to Sophia! Did you hear me?"

She hadn't. It was easy enough to figure out what she had been asked, though. All her mother cared about was appearances.

"I have a dress picked out," Sophia said as she moved to her walk-in closet, grabbing the light green chiffon dress that would match her eyes. It wasn't too revealing and swished with her body when she walked.

"You're kidding me? Don't be stupid, Sophia. You can't wear the same color as me."

One simple phrase.

Four meaningless words.

Her brain shut down.

Her body vibrated with pain.

Don't be stupid, Sophia.

You're so stupid.

Why do I have to have such a stupid child?

They're just words, *breathe*.

Sticks and stones, Soph.

So why did she feel like her heart was being ripped from her chest?

CHAPTER
ONE

YOU DON'T ALWAYS NEED A PLAN.
SOMETIMES YOU JUST NEED TO BREATHE,
TRUST, LET GO AND SEE WHAT HAPPENS.

"Ma." Lennox Hogan couldn't believe she'd dragged him and his two brothers, Levi and Lochlan, out for this. Building a garden two months too early. "It's not gonna work, Ma."

"Don't you 'Ma' me, young man. I want this garden done, and I want it done today. When I told you boys I was going to do it, you refused to let me. This," she swept her arm across the hole they'd dug, "was all your idea."

He really hated when she was right. They did refuse to let her do it, not wanting her to hurt her hip again after just losing her walking cane after her last fall. Her previous brilliant idea had been to paint the ceiling. His mother, the amazing woman who'd birthed him and his two younger brothers, a woman he respected more than anyone, decided to climb up a ladder, by herself, to paint a vaulted ceiling that even with the extension didn't mean she could reach the thirty feet needed. She'd fallen six feet to the ground, thus breaking her hip. He shuddered to think of what could have happened had she been at the top.

Now she had crates of roses in varying colors off to the side, anticipating planting them all that day. Leaving Nox and his brothers no choice but to finish digging the fucking hole and building the outer box and small path she wanted going straight through.

"C'mon, Ma, you can't be serious?" his youngest brother Lochlan groaned. At twenty-two years old, he was pretty sure the other man would rather be out at some park chasing tail on such a nice day. Not in his mother's garden.

Arching her brow, she sipped her sweet tea, pointedly putting her feet up as if to say, *get to it*, before grabbing the book she'd been reading. Some new romance she insisted she needed since she didn't have their father anymore. He passed four years ago from lung cancer.

When he'd first been diagnosed, his mother had been inconsolable, but within only a matter of hours, she knew they had to make the time they had left as amazing as they could. His father's cancer could have been manageable, but his quality of life would have been shit. Finding it at stage four, they knew they were going to lose him. It took nearly eight months for him to deteriorate right before their eyes. In that time, Nox and his brothers had sent them on the Alaskan cruise they had always planned to go on when they were older.

It was a memory their mother looked upon fondly now. She had taken as many pictures of him as she could. If someone came to her house, she was sure to show you them all whether you'd seen them a thousand times before or not.

Lennox grew up watching the love his parents had for one another, and from an early age, he always knew that would be his biggest goal in life. To love so hard that when your other half was gone, you could still live. Live to be the you they always knew you were.

He was a rough around the edges kind of guy, and at twenty-seven, he was aware that he still had time to find the right girl for him. His dad had always told him he'd know who she was because when he laid eyes on her, his palms would sweat and his heart would race so fast and hard it would feel like it was about to pound out of his chest. Plus, he'd say the dumbest thing he could. If that scared her away, then he'd have to work harder for her. If it didn't, then he'd be golden and know she would be perfect.

The brothers spent the afternoon digging and rototilling the sixteen by sixteen foot rose garden to be planted. Blood, sweat, and tears would be tossed in that sucker by each of them. Levi had blisters on all but four fingers, Loch had cried in relief when the rain started for about four point six seconds of relief, and he'd been sweating like a pig for hours. Owning the only specialty mechanics shop in town, you would think he should be used to working with the heat. Except in his garage, he had air conditioning. If his men saw him now, they'd be calling him all kinds of names.

"Sophia!" he heard his mother call happily.

Wiping his brow, he ignored her and her friend, wanting to just finish what they were doing. It wasn't until he noticed his brothers weren't working that he realized they were damn near drooling at something behind him.

Turning, the sun blinded him for a fraction of a second. Blinking away the spots in his eyes, he felt sucker-punched when he saw the beauty standing before him, cheerily chatting with his mother.

Whoa. She was the most beautiful thing he'd ever seen. Long blonde hair wind-blown into a messy style that looked like it took her hours to do, light green eyes that stood out with her natural red-tinted lips, topped off by a cupid's bow top lip. The fullness in her bottom lip made him want to nibble on it and see how long it would take to plump up to a bee-stung look.

She had an hourglass figure with wide hips meant for a man's hands to hold onto while he loved her from behind. Her cinched waist led to perky breasts perfect to fit in his palms. Not too big, and not too small. Her light yellow sundress drew his eyes to her in such a way that they couldn't focus on any one spot.

"Nox." Loch elbowed him just as the girls turned to them.

Checking for drool, Nox straightened his stance and dropped his shovel. He wasn't prepared for the impact her soft voice would have on him. "Umm, hi, I'm Sophia Bennett." She held out her hand, waiting for him to shake it, but all he could do was stare.

The prolonged silence had her fidgeting and slowly lowering her hand again, when one of his brothers coughed loudly in his ear, knocking him from his state of stupidity. "Sophia Bennett, as in Rebecca Bennett's daughter?" More stupidity spewed from his lips. He knew Mrs. Bennett because she had been bringing in her Mercedes sedan every other week with one fake problem or another. Lately, she had gotten handsier than he liked, so he was trying to avoid her like the plague.

The moment her mother's name came out of his mouth, though, Sophia paled and seemed to draw into herself. His mom caught it right away, knowing the trouble he'd been getting from her mother. She gave him a dirty look.

"Sorry, Soph, I'm Lennox, or Nox. It's a pleasure to meet you." His ma didn't live in the richer part of town, so he was confused as to what she was doing there. "What are you up to in our neck of the woods?"

Sophia's cheeks pinked with his rapt attention. "Lennox, she comes every Sunday and has tea with me, and we talk books," his mother admonished like he should already know.

He watched as Lorraine pulled sweet Sophia to the house, all the time wondering what her game was. It wasn't coincidence that she had tricked them all into coming over on that day he was sure.

"Who is she?" Levi whispered in wonder, completely smitten with the young woman.

"No clue. But I'd sure like to get to know her better." Loch smirked. He was the youngest of the three and an eternal flirt. Nox would have his fair share of laughs when the young man finally found his one.

Sophia, though? She wasn't it.

Because she was going to be his.

Every Sunday for more weeks than she could count, Sophia had been meeting with Lorraine Hogan to discuss new romance books they'd been reading. She had originally met the older woman in a used bookstore when she was combing through the shelves for something different than what she normally read. Which was usually whatever her mother chose. Classic books like Shakespeare.

It's not to say she didn't love Hamlet or Romeo and Juliet, but she wanted to read something that got her heart beating faster, made her palms sweat, and her heart ache for the passion read between the pages. Until Lorraine, she didn't think it could be something she would actually indulge in.

"What would you like to drink, dear?" the woman inquired as they entered her reading room. More like a library. The walls were filled with books of every genre from romance to thriller to murder mystery. Memoirs and classics, true crime mixed with old journals. There was nothing left untouched.

"A sweet tea, please, ma'am." Smiling unguardedly, Soph truly wished her own mother could be as loving.

"What have I told you about calling me ma'am, Miss Sophia?" There was laughter behind her words.

"I could do that when you started having grand-babies." She always had a wistful look in her eye when she spoke of her sons giving her babies again.

"That's right. Now, if only I could get them boys of mine to understand." A longing entered her gaze.

Finding a chance to be nosy about the one man that had captured her attention, Sophia asked, "Don't their wives or girlfriends want children?"

A snort of laughter left Lorraine before she could muffle it. "Those boys of mine," she began, holding her attention, "they're smart. They won't settle for anything less than perfect, and not a single one has found that perfect woman for them yet. Single!" she calls out laughingly. "All of them single."

Perfect?

Something Sophia wasn't.

Lennox had drawn her eye as soon as she saw the three strong men digging their mother a garden weeks too early. He had a hardness to him that she was drawn to. His strength oozed from his pores like armor.

His dark blue eyes paired with his light blond hair and dark scruff on his face made her heart stutter in her chest. It was that feeling she'd read about. The one she longed to experience. Only now, her dreams were dashed. Gone. Flying high in the clouds with the wind. She wasn't anywhere near perfect. She would never be what he wanted.

Especially if her mother knew him.

―――――――

Lorraine watched more emotion flit across young Sophia's face than she should even know how to feel. The first time she had seen the young woman, she felt a connection. She knew that they were meant to meet in the small bookstore that day but had no idea then how much poor Soph would need her now. Every week she came to Lorraine's home looking sadder and sadder. Slightly more broken.

It wasn't until she had been looking through old photos of her and her husband Lucas that she realized what Sophia needed. A wonderful, kind, caring, strong man. A man she could lean on. A man she could count on.

Luckily for Sophia, Lorraine happened to have three strong, strapping boys. All grown into the finest of men. Most definitely taking after their father.

Lennox, however, was the one she knew would be perfect for Sophia. He was such a rough man, all hard edges. He needed a soft woman to curve those edges a bit.

Sophia was that girl.

———————

Who is she?

It was all Nox could think about as he watched her walk inside with his mother. She'd captivated him, and he couldn't shake her loose. His brothers watched her, too, and he had this unexplainable urge to beat them both with the shovels they were holding. They'd fought over hundreds of things over the years, but never had a girl been one of them.

Never had he had such a strong compulsion to toss a woman over his shoulder and drag her away like a caveman. He wasn't that guy. He was laid back, took the hits as they came. Not once had he been so...jealous.

He was fucking jealous!

"Christ almighty," he cursed as he kept digging deeper than he was supposed to, so he had to go back and refill part of the hole.

"What's up your ass, bro?" Levi elbowed him in the ribs.

Shaking his head, Nox tried to ignore the not so

subtle jabs from his brothers. Didn't matter they had no clue what his mind was so wrapped up in. They only enjoyed tormenting him.

"You banging her mom?" Loch's question had his head popping up like a springboard.

"What the fuck did you say?" he bellowed.

Loch's eyes darted to Levi before slowly moving back to meet his. "I just meant, you know her mom, right?"

"Fuck you, Lochlan," he snarled.

"Lennox!" His mother's gasp could be heard a mile away he was sure.

"Ma–"

"Don't you 'Ma' me, young man. Watch your tongue, and we'll be fine." The anger in her voice shocked him until he turned around and saw Sophia standing on the porch with her.

The sunlight hit her in such a way that it was like a spotlight, and she was on display just for him so he could admire her beauty. Take her in a like a breath of fresh air.

Her light blonde curls framed her gorgeous face. Lips plump and begging for him to nibble on them, eyes so dark and expressive. He saw her confusion about his mother giving him shit, a small smirk playing on her succulent lips.

"It's alright, Lorraine," he heard her whisper.

"No. It's not. You keep those words for the shop, Lennox." Suddenly he was five years old again and sniffing his pop's whiskey glass.

"Whatever you say, Ma," he submitted.

Lorraine Hogan was what her friends called sweet as cherry pie. He called her a tyrant. She ruled the family home with an iron fist, and heaven help those that tried to defy her. If they were walking straight the next day, they were lucky sons of bitches.

"Why don't you boys come inside for some sweet tea?" she asked them with a Cheshire cat grin, and he knew she was up to something.

Nox was man enough to admit he should probably be scared.

Sophia's intoxicating aura held him a captive, willing audience, and he'd walk through hell to be closer to her. She refused to look any of them in the eye as they marched past her and his mom one by one. When he would have entered the house, he stopped in front of her. Wanting—no needing—their eyes to connect. To feel the punch in the gut he was sure he would get.

As her hands began to fidget, he could tell she was uncomfortable, and yet, he couldn't draw his intense gaze from her if he'd tried, which he didn't.

Not when his mother lightly touched his elbow in support—the sneaky witch—and not when she realized he was blocking her way into the house.

Once he was sure they were left alone, he whispered, "Sophia," letting her name roll off his tongue. Fuck did he ever love the sound of it on his lips.

He saw her dart a quick look up from below her lashes before her eyes shot to the ground again. Her breathing picked up, and she began rocking on the balls of her cute little pumps.

"How old are you, Soph?" She couldn't be over twenty, he'd swear on it.

"Nineteen," she murmured after clearing her throat.

He was internally pumping his fist while outwardly he smiled, still waiting for her to look up. Hoping his silence would unnerve her enough to finally meet his stare.

He'd have sworn she was about to say something when some fancy looking BMW pulled up to the curb, and her entire body tensed so hard he thought she might shatter.

"You okay, Soph?" He didn't recognize the vehicle, but she obviously did.

Nodding, she whispered sadly, "Please tell

Lorraine thank you for me," darting down the porch before he could say anything in response.

When the driver's side door opened and her mother stepped out, a string of curses flew from his lips. "Well, hello, Lennox," Rebecca purred, making him want to vomit. His eyes remained glued to Sophia, though, as she stopped in front of the car, shoulders slumped. "Why Sophia," she says loudly, "if I'd known you were coming for the view, I'd have joined you." Her sly smile didn't fool him.

"I read with Mrs. Hogan, Mother." Sophia's voice was robotic. It was eerie.

"Don't be so stupid, Sophia. We know Lennox is a better view."

He was disgusted with her. Absolutely repelled.

What he saw in Soph as she looked back towards him was what had him stepping forward. Her body wilted at her mother's words. Her eyes were cold and detached.

Lifeless.

"Soph?" he questioned as she began to climb into the back seat, completely ignoring him. The door closed with a soft snick just as he reached her. When he went for the door handle, her mother locked it.

"She's really not into men, Lennox," Mrs.

Bennett told him as she tried to slide her hands up his chest. Frowning when he pulled away from her slimy touch, she said to him, "How about you and I go out soon, huh?"

His eyes narrowed at her question. "You're married, Mrs. Bennett."

"Doesn't mean I can't have fun."

He couldn't deal with that woman. Dear God, did she have no shame? "Good-bye, Mrs. Bennett," he replied politely, aware his mother was watching, and slut or not, he knew she'd smack him if he said what he really wanted to.

When she got back in her car, his fingers automatically went to the rear window, wishing Soph would climb back out. Talk to him for a while. Closing his eyes as they pulled away, he imagined her fingers touching the same spot on the inside of the car.

"Fuck!" he screamed, unable to hold his frustration in.

When he turned to go back to the house, his family was standing there watching the whole exchange. "Don't, Ma," he told her softly, walking inside when she would have given him shit for swearing.

"I know, son," she whispered back. Obviously

aware of more than he was.

Nineteen. Sophia was an adult. So why did she feel like a child? Why couldn't she break free of the hold her mother had over her?

Stupid.

A word. Six simple letters.

Yet, they brought forth her biggest insecurities.

All of her pain sprang forth as soon as it passed her mother's lips. Every time she tried to assert her independence, her mother would tell her how stupid she truly was. How she wouldn't make it in the world without her.

As she sat in the back of her father's BMW, every one of her doubts raced forward at warp speed. She wanted out of her mother's clutches, only with no way to escape, she had no idea what to do. She had tried going to her father, but he had been no help. With the choice of a quiet home or facing her mother's wrath, he'd chosen to stay out of everything. Instead, locking himself away in his office for work or to drink. Sometimes both.

Looking back to Lorraine's house, to Lennox, she

wondered if maybe they could help her find her strength. Free herself from being unworthy.

It was an impossible dream nonetheless. She would never in a million years consider letting someone in on her home life. Watching her mother flaunt herself around town like a whore was bad enough. If they knew how weak she, herself, was, well, it was a shame she couldn't bear.

Her mother's glare in the reflection of the rearview mirror caught her attention. Unsure of what she'd done wrong, she remained quiet. "You stay away from him," she warned.

"Okay," she answered softly.

"He likes a refined woman," she gloated.

When Sophia didn't give the response her mother wanted, she continued on. "He doesn't like weak women." She refused to engage in her mother's tirade. "Stupid women don't attract him."

Bullseye.

Right in the heart.

The smile on her mother's face was disgusting. She enjoyed tormenting Sophia, and she failed to understand why.

"Why?" She summoned the courage to ask quietly.

Harsh laughter was her only response.

Watching as the town rolled by through her window, Sophia couldn't help wondering if maybe she really was stupid? She often missed social cues, couldn't read a person's mood, and generally just tried to keep out of the public.

"You never did understand what it means to be a Bennett, Sophia. You have to exude poise and grace." *And sleep with any willing dick.* Sophia didn't voice that out loud, of course. "You should be locked away. Seen, never heard." Her mother continued speaking, but she tuned her out.

Rebecca loved to hear her own voice. She was so self-involved that she didn't always notice when people insulted her. The way Lennox had. She'd just kept flirting and embarrassing herself.

Sophia often wondered why her parents were still together. They had slept in separate wings of the house for as long as she could remember. Only spoke to each other when it was necessary, which wasn't often. Neither had been affectionate towards each other that she'd ever seen.

Sometimes, when they didn't know she had been watching, her father would shoot daggers at her mother with his eyes, so much hatred lurking in their depths before he would shove it back into hiding. It would remain a mystery she supposed.

Her mother picking her up that afternoon had been a shock. She tried to avoid being seen in public with Sophia as much as possible. When her father's car had pulled up, she knew he wasn't in it. He always had a driver take him everywhere.

Lead had lined her stomach as her mother's perfectly made up legs slithered out first, followed by her perfectly botoxed face. Upon seeing Lennox, the light in the older woman's eyes turned predatory. Clearly and thankfully, he hadn't shared the same sentiments towards her.

Pulling into the driveway of their home, which was more like a mausoleum, Sophia was quick to exit the car. Racing up the front steps as her father and what she assumed was a client walked out the door.

"Where's the fire, Soph?" her father asked, confusing her. It was a rare and worrisome occasion when he acknowledged her in a client's presence.

Pausing, she wasn't sure what to do when his client offered a hand in introduction. "Pleased to meet you, Miss Sophia. I'm Braxton Hughes, an associate of your father's. He speaks highly of you."

The man, Braxton, seemed genuine. His eyes weren't cold like many of the men her father brought around. Her suspicions were raised because this was foreign territory for her.

"Don't be stupid, girl. Show some damn manners." Her mother's cold words were like a bucket of ice water tossed on her.

Unable to hide the pain from her face, she was able to mask her voice, at least. "My apologies, Mr. Hughes. It's a pleasure to meet Father's coworkers." She gingerly shook his hand, not wanting to be around for longer than was considered rude.

Unfortunately, he saw right through her; however, he kept it to himself since her parents were engaged in a glaring contest. "Do they do this often?" he whispered next to her ear. Closer than she liked.

Not thinking and still thrown off balance from the entire encounter, she replied back, softly, "It's a miracle they haven't clawed each other's eyes out yet."

His bark of laughter caught their attention and had her gasping in shock that she'd actually voiced her opinion.

"What did you say?" her mother hissed, taking a menacing step towards Sophia.

"Nothing that isn't true, Rebecca," her father, surprisingly, agreed. Mouth hanging open, she was stunned and confused. This entire encounter was playing on her already feeble nerves. She had no idea what was going on, but she didn't think she liked it.

"Anthony!" The woman's face turned an unnatural shade of purple. *Did she stop breathing?*

"Seriously, is it always like this?" Braxton asked, apparently amused by her strange family dynamics.

"Ummm, no?" Concern swarmed her as she saw her father quickly losing whatever good mood he was in as her mother continued her ranting.

"Enough, Rebecca!" he hollered at the older woman. Sophia took a step back as Braxton stood in front of her, trying to shield her from her father's wrath. "I'm sick of your tyrannical bullshit. Get yourself together or get out." Deafening silence met his words.

Noticeably shocked, Rebecca was mute for a quick second before glowering at her husband. Not saying a word to him, she turned on her heel towards the door, but not before stopping beside Sophia and whispering in her ear, "You useless twit. Stay away from Lennox, or you won't like what happens."

Sophia knew better than to show any signs of emotion, but she worried. Her mother had never threatened her before. *What is going on in my house?*

"Sophia?" Her father's sharp voice had her standing at attention.

"Yes, Father?" She stepped around Braxton's broad back.

"Braxton, here is your new detail."

Confusion hit her. "Detail? For what?"

"I've received a few threats, and I'd like to make sure you're protected. He'll be your shadow for a while." With that short explanation, he began to walk away.

Stepping forward, she grabbed his arm. "I don't understand. What's happening?"

The coldness she was used to was back in his hard eyes. "Nothing for you to worry about. Do as Braxton says, and everything will be fine."

"What about Mother?" she asked. Concerned even though the other woman unmistakably hated her.

"Don't worry about her." His words were soft, his hand gliding down her hair in a loving caress was once again confusing. "She'll be just fine." There was a flicker in his eyes. Something was going on that he didn't want to tell her.

"You'll be okay?" she asked quietly. He wasn't the most attentive father, but he'd shown her more love than her other parent, so she did care and wouldn't want anything bad happening to him.

"I'll be fine, Soph. Just stay with Braxton, please?"

"I promise."

She watched as he walked away to the Town Car waiting to take him wherever he went. Concern flowed through her. Something was happening with her parents, and she had the feeling she would become the only causality of their war.

CHAPTER TWO

LIFE IS NOT ABOUT WAITING FOR THE STORM
TO PASS, IT'S ABOUT LEARNING TO DANCE
IN THE RAIN.

A KNOT FORMED in Lennox's gut as soon as Sophia had rolled away with her mother the day before and hadn't let go. Something was happening and not having access to her was eating away at him.

A search through her mother's file had only shown the older woman's cell phone number, and he refused to call her. He had the feeling that if he showed his interest in Soph to her, life might get hellish for the younger Bennett woman.

He had their address so he could just stop by. Except it seemed a tad stalkerish to him, and he worried Soph's skittish attitude the day before might make her run. Staring at her address a bit longer, he debated what showing up at her doorstep might actually do.

"Ya know, you could actually just go there instead of staring at her address until your eyes cross." Levi walked into his office, butting his damn nose in where it didn't belong.

"Piss off, Levi," he snapped back.

Plopping down in the chair reserved for customers, his boots landing on Nox's desk, Levi continued on. "She might like it. Plus, you might actually get some work done instead of leaving it all to Loch and I."

"You're annoying as hell." Not paying attention to

what he was saying to his brother, he was giving serious thought to going to her house. She was sad when she left the day before, plus his mother was worried about her.

"I'm your little brother, I'm supposed to be. Now, will you please go see the girl. Loch and I are worried, too." His younger brother's voice was uncharacteristically serious as he spoke.

Without answering, Nox got up, grabbed his keys from the hook by the door, and took off for his 1964 Pontiac GTO. Levi could be heard as he slammed through the bay door in the garage. "Nice talking to you, too!"

Climbing into his classically built muscle car, Nox started her up and took off for Soph's. He had a good fifteen minutes' drive to plan what he was going to say when he got there and how he was going to deflect her mother if the woman was there as well.

The rumble of the 348hp Tri-power V-8 engine was music to his ears. He'd rebuilt the beauty with his father when he was sixteen and starting out as a classic car novice. The more they'd restored the vehicle, the more he'd fallen in love with engines of any kind. He had a real knack for rebuilding them and transmissions.

After tricking out the paint job on the beast in a beautiful Marimba red, he'd begun custom painting other vehicles around town in his parent's garage. Saving up to one day open his own business. It wasn't long before Levi and Loch had started investing their own time and money into helping him. After the summer that he'd turned eighteen, they all knew it was what they planned to do.

Four years, a business major, and a good investment later, and they'd successfully opened Hogan Bros.' Mechanics and Restoration. The first year of building up clientele had been rocky, but they'd made it through. Now they're booked months in advanced for restorations and weeks for regular mechanical maintenance.

There was the oddball emergency situation they took care of immediately, but thankfully, the two other mechanical shops in Loveland, Colorado picked up the overflow. Adding the restoration to their business removed the rivalry the other shops might have felt when he and his brothers opened theirs. Having a specialty meant they weren't looking to take over the day to day mechanical issues.

Growing up in the sleepy town, he'd seen many businesses try and fail and pop up again stronger than ever before. They were resilient citizens that he admired and was happy to provide a few jobs and bring in some tourism from his custom work.

He wondered how Soph would feel about him being a grease monkey. She was so put together, refined. Like fine china his mother only took out for the holidays. She hadn't spoken more than a fistful of words to him, so he had no idea how she was even going to react to him just showing up at her home.

Oh hell, have I turned stalker after five minutes in her presence?

He found he didn't care if he did. She was it for him. They had a lot to learn about each other, but he had faith they would.

She was the quiet to his outgoing. The soft to his hard. The sweet to his spicy.

And he was waxing poetic now.

Just fucking great.

He was tied up in knots over how she would accept his claim. Never before had he felt so unsure as he did right then.

As he pulled up to the mansion she lived in with her parents, he was shocked at just how massive it was. He wasn't poor by any means and hadn't grown up lacking for anything, however, being faced with the luxury she was used to was a kick to the nuts. If he couldn't give her everything she was used to, would she push him away? He wouldn't let her, of course. Come hell or high water she would be his. He would make them work.

Thankfully, no gates were denying him entry onto the estate. All seemed quiet as he parked under the porte-cochère at the front of the house. He was sure someone would have heard the rumble of his engine and was shocked Rebecca hadn't come running out.

Walking up the steps to her door, he noticed the grease stains on his hands as he went to ring the bell. Probably should have cleaned up a bit first.

Shrugging his shoulders, he rang the doorbell as an image of him dirtying Sophia up with those same hands entered his mind. To see her polished self abandon her roots, to let him sully her pristine image, had his cock growing at lightning speed.

Shit. He had to get himself under control. Thinking hockey stats, he hoped it would help before anyone answered. "Can I help you?" The door. *Shit.*

"I'm looking for, Soph," he told the older man. He was dressed like a butler maybe? Did people still have butlers?

"Soph?" he questioned.

Is he for real?

"Sophia," Nox clarified.

"Ahh, the young Miss Bennett. She's not taking visitors." The man's indifference bothered him. He just wasn't sure why.

"Not taking visitors," he asked. "She doesn't even know I'm here."

"I assure you, no visitors."

He'd had enough of the man. "Sophia!" he yelled into the house, hoping she'd hear him wherever she happened to be.

Another man came into view. He looked as though he belonged in the house as much as Lennox did. Tall, around his own age of twenty-seven, Nox figured he had to be security. No way anyone living in the house had tattoos like the hardened man.

"Can I help you?" he asked after eyeing Nox up and down.

"Where's Soph?" he asked a-fucking-gain.

The two men said a couple words quietly to each other before the maybe butler left the room. He wasn't even paying attention anymore because he could hear soft steps coming closer and knew it was his girl. No way would her mother walk around barefoot.

As Sophia came around the corner at the top of the stairs, eyes wide and frightened, he forgot any manners his mother had instilled in him and booked it up the stairs faster than the might be security guy could catch him.

A small smile lit her face as he reached her, but the fear was still there. His hands immediately went to her curvy hips.

Fuck do they feel good in my hands.

"Soph," he sighed just before his lips landed on hers in a light kiss. He couldn't help it. They were soft, pliable, and willing.

Mine.

The spark he felt down to his soul cemented everything he'd been feeling the past twenty-four hours. She was his, and he was hers.

"Lennox," she sighed happily as he pulled away.

Before he could respond, a hand landed on his shoulder, spinning him around. He came up swinging more out of reflex than assessing any real threat. As his fist connected with the might be security guy's jaw, a shocked gasp left Sophia's tender lips.

"Dude!" the other man called, shocked by Nox's response.

"Don't fucking grab a guy, *dude*," he snarled back. He had no idea who the fucker was or why they weren't allowing him to see his girl.

Ignoring the interloper again, he looked to Sophia whose eyes were wide in shock. "What's going on, Soph?" he demanded.

Her eyes skittered to his, so many emotions swirled in their lightness. "I don't know," she finally whispered, stepping back.

"Who the hell are you?" the man he'd punched snapped out.

"Who am I?" Nox scoffed. "Who the fuck are you? And why the fuck are you in my woman's house?"

"Your woman?" The man latched on to his inference.

Shit.

No point in backing out now. "Yeah. Mine. Now, who are you?"

Nox looked between the pair for so long he didn't think anyone was going to answer him.

"I was hired to protect Sophia," the bodyguard replied.

Not fond of the other man saying her name, Nox decided to question the first part of his statement. "Protect?"

"Someone's been threatening my father. Braxton was hired to shadow me," Soph answered when the other man wouldn't.

37

"Braxton?" he questioned her. Her cheeks flamed pink, and he had to kiss her again. Stalking towards her, she back-stepped away from him. Lucky for him, his legs were longer, and he reached her before she could run.

His arms bracketed her shoulders as he leaned into her slowly, giving her time to pull away or tell him to stop. Shockingly, she licked her lips, and when he looked into her eyes, he saw the need reflected back at him.

"Fuck yeah," he murmured as he descended on her.

She tasted like cherries. Sweet as he entered, tart as he explored. Her lips opened willingly when he nipped her lower lip lightly. Her hands shot to his chest, rubbing gently as he devoured her light moans. Deepening the kiss, his body pressed hers as close to the wall as he could manage without burying himself inside of her. When he finally got that chance, it wouldn't be in the middle of a hall with an audience. It would be in his bed with her screaming his name until her voice was hoarse.

A clearing throat had him slowly pulling away from her tasty lips. He could kiss her for hours and never get bored.

"You two done yet?" Braxton asked, impatience evident in his voice.

Lennox's eyes never left Sophia's as he pulled away. The embarrassment reflecting back at him had him snapping, "What?", at the man behind him.

"Why are you here? And who the fuck are you?"

Were they in a fucking merry-go-round or what?

Knowing he had to curb his desire to flatten the man in order to get the information he wanted about why Soph needed a bodyguard, he hissed out, "Lennox Hogan. I'm obviously here for Sophia."

Finally turning, he saw the fist-sized bruise forming on Braxton's face and smirked. Knowing he'd taken the man off guard left Nox insanely satisfied. "I've answered your question, now tell me what the fuck is going on that she needs a bodyguard."

"Braxton, could you excuse us, please," Soph asked quietly from behind him.

Hearing Lennox scream her name a few minutes after the doorbell rang had been shocking. Her mother had warned her away from the man, and she found it hard to believe he was there for her. Yet, he was. The way he'd sunk his entire body against hers, devoured her untried mouth, proved it. It was almost too much to believe. After all the griping her mother had been doing the day before, she made it seem like she and Lennox were an item. That he was hers.

She was so conflicted.

Which had Sophia blurting out, "My mother's not here," before she could think it through. She wanted to smack her own head.

The narrowing of her visitor's eyes showcased the storm brewing in his mind.

"Did it just feel like I was here for that cold-hearted wench to you?" The anger in his voice made her wish she could escape. She didn't do well with confrontation.

Should have kept your mouth shut then.

"I'm sorry," she whispered to him.

Ignoring her apology, he went straight to the heart of her problems. "What's going on, Sophia? Ma never mentioned you were in danger."

"I didn't know I was." Fear had been her companion since her father's revelation, and she still didn't understand what was going on. Braxton wasn't budging. Her father hadn't been home since dropping his bombshell and leaving. And she'd been avoiding her mother by staying in her room.

"I don't understand, catch me up."

"When I got home yesterday, mother and father had a fight," she began, still confused about the entire exchange.

"And you're in danger because of that?"

She couldn't help the smile that played on her lips from his own confusion. He got these cute wrinkles in his forehead that she wanted to smooth out.

"No. Because of father's work," she said. "I think."

"What do you mean, you think?"

"Lennox?" Sophia cringed at hearing her mother's nasally voice, not realizing the woman had come home. "How nice of you to come by." His face went from confused to annoyed to angry in a flash.

"Not here for you, ma'am," he told her mother without even turning to face the wretched woman.

Her mother, however, was not swayed. "Well, who else would you be here for?" She obviously didn't know or care that her daughter was being blocked by his body.

Looking over his shoulder, Sophia shuddered at the anger in his eyes. "Sophia," he responded to the older woman.

Rebecca's entire demeanor changed with that one word. She didn't have to see the woman to know she was in for a ton of trouble when he left. "Why would you want her?" Pain sliced through Sophia's chest.

Lennox turned to fully face the woman, and Sophia decided she didn't want or need to hear any more, so she began to slowly slither her way down the hall to her room. Closing her door with a quiet snick, she could hear her mother's raised and frantic voice as Lennox tried to back out of whatever it was she wanted.

Leaning against her door, taking deep breaths, she tried to force the tears back. She would not cry over something that was never hers. She always knew she would be stuck in her family home. Why had never even been a thought. It just was what it was.

When she met Lorraine Hogan, she experienced hope for the first time. Hope for more, for a life. For something. Sophia had never been encouraged by her parents when she was in school; she was never a straight A student. She was lucky that she had a C average.

Her mother had always been more concerned about appearances than grades or school. Sophia became a pretty little doll for her to dress up. Never a real daughter. Now, as an adult, she felt less than useless. While she had attended some of the finest schools in the state, she was never given the choice of going to college and becoming something. Real fear coursed through her body as she thought about how worthless of a person she was to society. With nothing to offer the world, she was a waste of space.

Pounding on her door had her thoughts disappearing and her heart rate skyrocketing. Turning slowly, she pulled the door open an inch to see an infuriated looking Lennox on the other side.

Pushing the door open, he forced his way in before shutting it with his foot and reaching back to lock it. All of this without taking his eyes off of her. When his hands came up to hold her face in a gentle grip, she was shocked to feel him wiping tears from her cheeks. She hadn't even realized she was crying.

"What's this?" he asked quietly.

Looking at the tear sitting on his thumb, she had no answer. "I don't know."

"You know I despise that woman, right?" His voice demanded she know the truth.

"I do," she murmured. *Now*, she silently added.

"Good," he mumbled just before drawing her face closer to his and capturing her lips in another searing kiss of passion. She'd never been touched by a man before, let alone experience the scalding hot desire he awoke inside of her.

It was over almost as quick as it started. "Damn," Lennox whispered against her lips. She was still frozen in place, unsure of what she should or shouldn't be doing.

"Go out with me." His quiet command startled her eyes into opening. The eagerness in his stare had her nodding her head without thought. His smile was reward enough for her.

"I've got some work to do tonight, so I'll pick you up at six tomorrow, yeah?"

"Okay." She found herself easily agreeing if only to see the happiness on his face. When he went to leave, she found the courage to ask the second person in as many days as to why.

His eyes fixed on the door for a full minute before he answered. "Because I need you." His answer was so simple, yet so unexplained. He clearly understood her question. The pain behind it. "You'll see, Soph. Real soon you'll see." Confused by his answer, she watched him walk away before throwing herself on her bed.

She'd never done anything like what Lennox wanted before. Her mother had never given her that chance, let alone the choice to be around boys. With more than twenty years separating them, Sophia always felt like her mother was competing with her for the affections of boys she didn't even have any interest in.

When Lennox had asked if she were her mother's daughter, she'd felt sick to her stomach imagining the first man she was attracted to being in any kind of relationship with the older woman. The thought had nearly sent her running for the hills.

Now, she wished for so many things, she didn't even know where to start. Lennox had a rough, hard exterior, but with her, he was soft and kind. He made her want things she'd never thought about.

Leaving Sophia in that house with that vile woman made Nox wish she wouldn't have freaked out if he'd taken her with him. He could almost count the minutes they'd spent in each other's company, and already, he was hooked. She was his drug of choice, and nothing else would do.

As he drove back to his shop, he thought of all the things he could do with her on their date. Then he thought of all the things she would actually like to do with him. His mother might be useful to recruit for help on it. After leaving her house the day before, he knew she had wanted one of them to click with Sophia when they met her. There was no doubt in his mind about it. She was constantly pestering each of them to meet a girl, settle down, give her some grandbabies. Undoubtedly, she had now taken it upon herself to play cupid.

Since she wanted to be a matchmaker, he'd put her to use. Clicking the Bluetooth on his phone, he called her number, hoping she would be home and not at one of her many card clubs she went to since his father's passing.

"Lennox, dear. What a lovely surprise." Her voice was cheerful, knowing. She'd been expecting to hear from him since his abrupt departure after Soph left.

"Hey, Ma, how you doing?" He'd worm his way into her helping if he had to.

"Oh, cut the bull, Lennox. What do you need?" She always could see right through them.

"I went and seen Soph today," he began.

She, of course, had to interrupt him. "That's wonderful, dear. Tell me the wicked witch of the west hasn't hurt her." She had his full attention now.

"What do you mean hurt her, Ma?" Rebecca was a total cunt, but he had a hard time believing she would do anything harmful towards another human. Then again, looks could be deceiving. He knew that better than most.

"Not physically, dear, calm your horses down. Her words can cut sharper than any knife, though. Sometimes poor Sophia comes here looking so sad and lost." That didn't make him feel any better.

"Son of– "

"Don't you dare say it, Lennox," she warned before he could finish his sentence.

"Sorry, Ma. Look, I do need your help, though. With two things." He was hoping she could find out more about what Soph's father did, and why she might be in danger.

"How can I help?"

"I'm taking Soph out tomorrow. Any ideas what she'd like?"

"A picnic!" she shot back immediately. He should have expected something of the sort.

"Okay, great. Chances you'll put that together are...?" *Fingers crossed*.

"I have the perfect idea!" *Thank God*.

"Now, the other thing...she has a bodyguard, Ma." Her sharp intake of breath indicated her shock.

"What for?" Fear was evident in her voice.

"That's the thing, all she knows is that her father has been getting some threats. I was hoping you could talk to some of Dad's old army buddies, maybe they can dig something up?"

"Of course! I'll call Sophia this afternoon, see how she's doing. Maybe I can convince her to come to knitting club tomorrow." The thought made the older woman happy.

"Sure, Ma, just don't come on too strong, will ya?" False hope he knew.

"Yeah, yeah, gotta go. Love you!" Barely giving him time to say goodbye and she was gone.

Back at the shop, he figured he might as well enlist his younger brothers' help as well. "Levi, Loch, in my office!"

He didn't see them in the bay but knew they'd hear him and come. It wasn't often he called to them for a meeting. Barely past the doorway and they came crashing through like a barrel of monkeys.

"'Sup?" they asked at the same time.

"What is with you two? You suddenly become twins or what?" They hated when he asked them that. As close as they all were, they each despised being compared to the other.

"Sophia's dad thinks she might be in danger." No point in mincing words.

"What do you need?" Levi asked. Nox knew he could count on them.

Thinking about the question, he didn't even know what to say. "I have no fucking clue." She had a bodyguard who seemed capable enough. "I need you guys to search around. Find out if anything is going on in town we don't know about." They nodded their agreeance and pulled out their phones to call or text someone they thought could help. "It needs to be on the low-low, guys. Her dad's a security guy for some significant criminal law firm. I'm thinking it's probably one of the pissed off clients."

"You got it," Loch responded as they began walking back into the shop.

The thought of something happening to Sophia because her father protected criminals pissed him off in a huge way. She was too soft, sweet, innocent to be tainted by such evil. She should be cherished in all manners.

He would make sure she was if it was the last thing he did.

CHAPTER THREE

TAKE EVERY CHANCE.
DROP EVERY FEAR.

WHEN SOPHIA'S alarm clock went off in the morning, she wanted to throw it across the room. She had spent most of the night locked away in her room listening to her parents express more emotion towards each other than she could remember happening. Ever.

They fought for so long, she didn't think it would end, and they wouldn't go to another part of the house. She didn't learn anything new about why she was possibly in danger, either.

She did learn she was a mistake.

Dumber than dirt.

A waste of air.

All her mother's words, of course. Nothing she hadn't been told a thousand times before. Nothing that hurt any less each time she heard it. Her father did his best to ignore her mom. She didn't expect the man to defend her. There was no defending against anything Mother said, but just once, she wished he had.

He'd changed over the past few years, became colder, harder. There was an edge to his temper that never used to be there. He was always kind to Sophia growing up, now though, it was as though he'd become robotic.

Living at home had become a burden she didn't

think she wanted anymore. Unfortunately, with having no experience in anything, it wasn't like leaving was exactly an option, either. But she had to figure out something. She couldn't keep going through the same insults and fights.

Her mother was getting more vicious with her words, and there was something in her eyes. Almost as though she was a missile just waiting to go off. The woman had never been kind, not that Sophia could remember, anyway; however, the last few months she had been as explosive as dynamite, and that scared her. She wouldn't put anything past the older woman. Not anymore.

Climbing from bed, she went straight to her small en suite, going through a quick shower. While blow drying her hair, an incoming text had her phone buzzing across her nightstand. Only four people had her number. Her parents, Lorraine, and now Braxton. Since she knew Braxton was probably downstairs waiting on her to wake up, she didn't think it was him. Her parents never bothered to text —usually, they just yelled for her, expecting her to come running like an obedient lap dog. She didn't think Lorraine had ever texted her. She just called, preferring to speak instead of waiting on an answer.

Confused as to who it could be, she slowly

walked over to the device, nervous about who would be on the other end. All the secrecy behind her father's suspicions were playing with her mind.

Grabbing the phone as it vibrated again, she nearly jumped out of her skin. The displayed message made her wish she could.

Frozen in place, fear coursing through her veins, she read the message over and over until the words began to blur together.

Soon, my pretty Sophia, you'll be mine.

The words themselves weren't so scary, it was the intent behind the words she feared. Maybe it was someone she knew, or perhaps it was someone trying to prank her. With so many what ifs and possibilities, she had no idea what to do. How to proceed.

The phone vibrated in her hand again and made her jump and drop it, bouncing it right under the bed. Slowly bending down, she dreaded reading the new message.

Device in hand, she kept one hand over the screen as she stood to sit on the edge of her bed. Unhurriedly, she uncovered the screen.

Her screams rent the air as black dots clouded her vision.

Don't look so scared, sweet Sophia, it won't hurt.

Braxton came crashing through her room, face hard as stone, gun in hand, ready to blast away her tormentor. Too bad he couldn't do anything.

"Sophia?" he questioned, his eyes searching the room.

Holding out her phone with a shaking hand, she waited as he took it. The change in him was immediate. On guard, pissed off, and ready to kill. His eyes swore vengeance.

"What's happening, Braxton?" She had to know. She couldn't be left in the dark anymore.

Gaging by the look in his eyes, whatever he was about to say was going to be a lie. "I don't know."

"Bullshit!" she yelled at him, her temper finally getting the best of her. "You do know. You don't strike me as the type of man to not have all the information you need for a job."

His lips were sealed tight. Something was happening, and her father didn't want her to know what. That was alright, she'd find out. She would push until someone told her.

Until then, though, she responded, "Fine. But me being uninformed could very well mean life or death. Do you really want that on your conscience?"

Guilt could be a great motivator for some people. While she didn't think she could guilt Braxton into telling her everything, a few answers just might be enough to find out what was going on.

She hoped.

Son of a motherfucking bitch.

The little spitfire had Braxton stuck between a rock and a hard place. She reminded him so much of his own sister with her meek presence, yet hellfire eyes. Her father had been very clear that she couldn't know what was happening. Why she was in danger.

That it had nothing to do with his work.

The threats had been clear from the beginning. Someone wanted Sophia. Their obsession with the young woman had become so compulsive that her father had hired him long before she'd met him.

He'd been tailing her for weeks when the threats got to be more graphic. Details of what the perpetrator wanted to do to her. Would do to her when he got his hands on her.

Anthony had been clear on two things when he'd hired Brax.

Keep Sophia safe at all costs.

Don't trust his wife.

Not telling Sophia about what was actually happening when she'd asked was hard as hell. Especially now that contact had finally been made with her. Shit was about to hit the fan, and frankly, he needed her to be aware of what was happening.

Knocking on Anthony's office door with Sophia's phone in hand, he knew it was time to have a word with the older man about not protecting her from the truth.

Avoiding everyone all day had seemed like a good idea after her showdown with Braxton earlier that morning over the threats against her father. Or her. Or whoever the hell was being threatened.

Sophia had been a nervous wreck all day. She'd tried playing music loud enough so that she wouldn't hear the creaks and groans of the house. It didn't work too well. Paranoia quickly reared its ugly head, and she feared not hearing someone coming —being taken by surprise.

When she shut the music off, she'd picked up a new romance book. Turns out it was a thriller romance with a lot of detail, and her imagination started running rampant. A text to Braxton confirmed that both her parents had left the house and weren't expected back anytime soon, so she'd gone to the family garden.

Filled with rows upon rows of roses, sunflowers, lilacs, and many other flora, it was normally her calming place. Sophia absolutely loved working in the garden, feeling the soil between her fingers as she gave life to the purest beauty.

Between birds chirping and the large bushes, trees, and shrubs, her own shadow became her worst enemy. She saw menace around every corner. Unable to enjoy herself for long, she'd taken solace back inside her room.

Behind a locked door.

Under a multitude of blankets.

Imagining the worst to happen.

Finally exhausted from the stress of her anxiety, she'd fallen into a panic-riddled sleep full of monsters and shadows. With no way to protect herself, she was soon entrapped in a nightmare made from horror flicks.

Cruising through the streets of town, anticipation and excitement flowed through Nox as Shinedown's "Call Me" blared through the speakers of his car on his way to pick up Soph. It had been a long time since he'd wanted to actually date a woman, get to know her.

With Sophia, there was something about her. She emitted this aura, a mystery he wanted to unlock. She wasn't just some dolled up society girl. There were layers to her, and he couldn't wait to peel each one back. Expose all of her.

Watching the clock all day made the time feel as though it was going backwards instead of forward. Work wasn't happening, so Loch and Levi had been forced to pick up his slack, not that he hadn't done the same for them in the past. This was a first for him, though, and they both had a blast busting his balls about it.

Leaving work early had been a blessing. Spending nearly an hour picking what he was going to wear had not been his proudest moment. It was her, all her. He wanted to be his best. Not because he thought she would expect more from him, he just got the feeling she cared more about who a person was rather than what they could offer. He wanted to look his best for her.

After staring at himself in the mirror for almost half that time wearing slacks, a dress shirt, and sport coat—which wasn't his style at all—he'd finally cursed up a storm and decided to go with his typical attire. A dark blue Henley paired with his lucky dark wash Buffalo jeans and bomber jacket over top. The coat might be a bit much since the spring weather was warming up.

It was purely selfish reasoning behind his choice. If Soph got cold, then she'd have to wear his coat, be surrounded by his scent. She'd go to sleep smelling of him.

The thought put a smile on his face. Simply thinking of her did that as well. She was a lightness he hadn't even realized his life was missing.

When he neared her neighborhood, the houses slowly grew larger, more ostentatious in appearance. Hers wasn't the most outlandish one he'd seen. It actually reminded him of a show home in some ways. The lawns were manicured to perfection, not a speck of grass out of place. No pebbles or leftover snow and dirt from the winter on the driveway. No cracks in the steps. Even inside, it was all show and shine. Everything sparkled like Mr. Clean's bald head.

Except her room.

Soph's room was the only one in the house he'd seen that had any life in it. She had bookshelves filled to the brim. Knick knacks and pictures strategically placed with love. It represented her in all its glory.

As he shut the car off, the house seemed darker than it had the day before. Quiet. Walking up the steps, he was about to ring the bell when the oak door opened slowly, Braxton stepping out.

Annoyance coursed through him. He understood the other man had a job to do, but it didn't mean he had to be a dick about it.

"Braxton," he greeted, trying to keep the peace.

"We need to talk." The guy pulled no punches.

"About?"

"Sophia." He had Nox's full attention.

"She's a bundled mess today. Full of nerves. I actually haven't seen her in a few hours." There was genuine concern in the other man's words.

"She in her room?" He wasn't going to wait around and talk; he'd get to her. At Braxton's nod, he was through the door and up the stairs before the man could move out of his way.

Reaching her door, he gave a slight knock, calling, "Sophia, it's Lennox." When there was no answer, he tried the door knob.

Locked.

Bending down, he inspected it, seeing it was a weak lock, and he could probably shoulder his way in if he wanted. Instead, he slipped a credit card from his wallet. Wiggling it between the jam and the door, he had it open not long after.

At first, he didn't know what he was looking at. The room seemed empty, bathroom was empty, curtains shut tight, and a bundle of blankets piled high on the bed was all there was. When a light moan and slight movement came from the bed, he understood. Not entirely, but enough to know where she was. Just not why.

Peeling the blankets back one at a time, he finally found her, overheated and sweating. Knots in her brow, eyes tightly closed as if she were warding off a bad dream.

Slipping his coat and boots off, he slid under the light sheet with her. His arms wrapped her against his body, and he softly called her name a few times before her frame relaxed into his embrace.

Gazing around her room, he tried to see what could have her in such a state when his eyes landed on Braxton standing in the door watching them.

"What happened?" he asked the other man.

At first, Brax was reluctant to speak, but he must

have seen the fortitude in Lennox's eyes; he wouldn't give up. "She received a couple of texts this morning. Threatening in nature, but nothing serious."

His cavalier attitude pissed Nox off. "What the fuck do you mean nothing serious? She's obviously freaked the fuck out. What did they say?" *What the fuck is going on?*

Sighing, Brax replied, "From an admirer, they would have been flattering. From a stalker, they're downright dangerous."

If comforting Sophia wasn't so fucking important, he'd take the ass out back for a beat down for his lack of a committed answer. "Get me on the same page you are, Braxton, quickly."

"We're still investigating, getting warrants, everything is still very preliminary."

"What the fuck does that mean?" he shouted, making the precious bundle in his arms flinch.

"It means," a new voice from the doorway spoke, "we can't confirm anything right now." The man entering the room was older, had Sophia's eyes, looked tired.

"You're her father?" he spat out.

"Yes." Just that, nothing else.

Nox had a bone to pick with the man about the way his wife treated her, only it would have to wait until he had all the information he could about whoever was stalking his woman.

"What can you confirm?" His joyful attitude from earlier had fled the moment he saw Braxton at the door.

"Not much."

He felt like they were going around in circles with the lack of answers he was getting. "What's the plan then? To wait? Let something happen?" Nox expected some type of reaction from her father about the possibility that harm might befall his daughter, the lack of one was troubling. "That's what you're going to do, isn't it?"

A look was shared between the two men before her father answered, "Don't be ridiculous. We're doing everything we can."

Like hell they were.

"Who do you think is doing this?" He didn't think he'd get an answer, but the pained look in her father's eyes led him to believe the man knew who he suspected on a personal level.

"I won't say until I know for sure," was his only answer before leaving the room, a look of regret on his face. Braxton followed before Nox could ask any more questions.

With as many secrets as the Kardashian's, he

wasn't sure he would get a straight answer from either man, even if they did know.

Sophia's sleep had been restless and full of monsters that went bump in the night. No one to save her. No one to hear her cries for help.

Until his warmth.

She was surrounded by musk and man.

His strength could be felt in her nightmares as he held her through her own personal storm. When she'd heard voices, it was hard to remain quiet. Hearing Braxton confirm she had a stalker was astonishing.

She had to be one of the most boring people in town. It wasn't as though she went out of her way for attention. She was always quiet when she went anywhere. The only real friend she had was Lorraine, and she highly doubted the older woman was stalking her.

When her father hesitated to answer Lennox's question, she suspected he did know who was behind the sudden threat, but probably wanted it to go away like any other problem.

She often wondered if he felt the same way

about her. Was she more of a burden now that she was older? Feeling insecure where her father was concerned was new. His distance the past few years had hurt. Burying it deep inside only made it worse.

"Soph?" Lennox whispered in her ear, breaking her free of her thoughts.

Opening her eyes, she looked into the pools of his midnight blues. Concern lit them as he searched her own.

"You doin' okay?" He obviously knew she'd been awake, or at least suspected.

"Tired." Her voice cracked from lack of moisture.

Slipping free of the bed, he held out a hand for her. "Come on, let's get you some fresh air and food."

"But what about...?" She couldn't say it out loud, it would make the whole scenario all too real.

"I won't let anything happen to you." His vow was comforting.

Taking his hand, she squeezed lightly as she walked past his tall frame to her en suite. Splashing water on her face to get some color back in her cheeks, she prayed everyone was wrong. That she didn't have a stalker, that she wasn't possibly in any danger. Her gut said otherwise, but her mind was all too delighted to believe it was possible.

Shaking off any and all thoughts of bad things to

come, Sophia wanted to enjoy her time with Lennox. She didn't want the stress of a threat. She didn't want the condemning tone of her mother in her head. She wanted, for once, to go on a date. She wanted to not be the weird rich girl in town.

She wanted simply to be known as Sophia. The shy, sweet girl, the girl who would give a stranger the shirt off her back if they needed it more than her.

In all honesty, she didn't even want to be Sophia anymore. People pitied that girl.

"Soph?" Lennox's strong voice gave her tingles in places she'd never thought about before.

Opening the door, she smiled shyly at him. "I'm ready." Though she hadn't done anything other than splash her face with water and run a brush through her hair.

If her mother could only see her now. She'd have a coronary for sure.

The thought made her giggle.

"What's so funny?" he asked her.

Still too shy to give him honesty, she said, "Nothing," before leading the way from her room. Amazed that he cared about her enough to stay with her in her time of need.

"What are we doing?" she asked as they descended the long staircase to the front door. Relief swamped her when neither of her parents intruded on them.

"Well, I thought we could go to some Italian restaurant my mother recommended downtown." She looked down at her clothes, her light purple sundress was wrinkled and not at all date material. Indecision had her looking back up the stairs. "But then I thought..." He ignored her look as he pulled her into his arms. He was always doing that. "I'd love nothing more than a nice picnic in the park. To see your beautiful eyes light up under the stars."

Her gaze widened at his sweet talk. No one had said such nice things to her before. "Oh my," she whispered in awe.

His charming smile drew her attention to the small dimple in one cheek as he leaned down to lightly kiss her lips. "Mmmm," he moaned pulling away. "So soft. So sweet." His words made her blush.

Not waiting a second longer, he guided her to his beautiful red car in the driveway. He clearly took pride in the machine with how spotless it was. Or maybe he cleaned it up for her? The thought had butterflies in her stomach going wild.

"I have a dress this same color," she whispered, running a delicate finger along the hood.

Leaning into her back, he grumbled in her ear,

"One day, I'll have you splayed out on top of the hood in that very dress." Her eyes closed at the tantalizing thought. "My head buried between your lush thighs." She froze in anticipation of his next words. "My name spilling from your delicious lips into the night." Her head went dizzy with lust as he helped her sit and buckled her in.

A smirk graced his face as he walked around the hood of the car to enter the driver's side. Clearly pleased with himself, the car started with a loud rumble before they were off to some unknown destination.

All she could think about was the picture he'd painted in her mind.

He wouldn't really do it, would he?

Fuck me six ways from Sunday. Why did you do that to yourself, Nox? The picture he'd painted of Sophia spread out on the hood of his car was all he could think about now. Her naked pussy wide open for his tasting pleasure, her cries in the night air for his ears only. It was an image he would have to make sure happened. He couldn't not experience that with her. He suddenly wished he'd allowed her to go back inside to change.

She wasn't ready for that yet, though. She was barely ready for him crashing into her life. He doubted she could handle all the depraved things he'd like to do to her on their first date. He'd have to warm her up to the idea of surrendering her pleasure to him. Of taking everything he had to give her without giving it back. It was all he wanted to do, he wanted her in a permanent state of orgasmic bliss before he took anything for himself.

When she's ready, Nox. He had to keep reminding himself of that. He had no clue what was going on with her at home, but he intended to find out on their date. She was single-handedly the shyest person he'd ever met. Not just people shy either, but life shy. Like she expected the world to kick her in the teeth at every turn. He hated seeing that.

The quiet in the car was screwing with his mind. While he knew she wasn't like any other woman he'd been with, she had to be the quietest woman he'd ever met.

"What do you like to do for fun, sugar?" His question seemed to startle her.

"Fun?" she asked like it was a foreign concept.

"Yeah, fun. What do you do to relax? Kill time?

Fun." His eyes darted between her and the road as she contemplated his question like he'd asked her to solve the Big Bang Theory.

"Oh, umm, I read sometimes. I volunteer at charities." Her response sounded more like questions than answers.

"You asking me, sugar, or telling me?" He smiled at her, hoping to get one in return.

No such luck.

"Telling?" Again, like a question.

"Soph." It was hard to imagine such a sweet creature like her not having something for herself. "What about friends? Do you like shopping with them, maybe a weekly lunch?"

"Friends..." The word sounded foreign on her tongue even to him. As though she rarely said it.

He remained quiet the rest of the drive, all the while watching her. Trying to gauge her mood to what he'd asked. He thought, for sure, it was a safe topic. Now he wondered even more about what the hell happened in her house.

They drove in silence to the park, his mind going a million miles a minute. There was so much about her that he thought he knew, and unfortunately, he had misjudged her because of who she was. Now, he had to make up for it. Get to know the real her, find out who she was, what made her tick.

From the corner of his eye, he watched her fingers fidget in her lap, giving away her nerves. Pulling her hand into his, he placed it on his thigh with his own overlapping it. Rubbing slow circles along the side of her wrist, he felt her finally relax.

"What, um, what do you like to do for fun?" she quietly asked him. A blush crept up her cheek, and he fucking loved it.

"My brothers and I restore old cars. We love the classics. This one here, our dad helped me rebuild from the chassis up." He smiled remembering the fun they'd had doing it.

"Did you always want to be an, uh, um, mechanic?" The way she stumbled over her words was far more adorable than he'd have ever imagined.

"Yeah, sugar, cars were all I cared about for a long time." He flashed her a bright smile as she squeezed his thigh.

Her smile was wanton as she said, "That must be nice." Her voice was wistful, as though she didn't know what that felt like. To have that kind of passion over something.

He'd give her something to be passionate about soon enough.

"Do you go to college?" he asked when she remained quiet again.

She turned her head towards the window, but not before he saw the sad look on her face. "No, I wasn't smart enough." She said it so matter-of-factly like there was no question about her lack of intelligence.

"I find that hard to believe."

"I was never cut out for school, anyway." Her voice wobbled at the end.

Reaching over to her, he gripped the back of her neck before pulling her to him. She shocked him when she unbuckled her belt, sliding across the bench seat to sit next to him. The light blush that was forever on her cheeks turned a deep red as she looked at him. She must have seen the heat in his eyes as she clicked her seatbelt into place once more.

Wrapping his arm around her shoulders, he played with her long ponytail, twirling strands around his finger as they arrived at the park.

"Here we are," he announced with an enthusiastic grin.

"Wow!" She marveled, her eyes lighting up at seeing the clear blue Colorado skies and snow-capped mountains in the distance. Wildflowers as far as the eye could see. All he could picture was

Sophia spread out in the grass, her skirt around her waist as he pleasured her with his mouth. Her screams would float away with the wind.

Nox watched the wonder cross her features as she took in the sight before them. Her gaze lit up with amazement as she watched birds fly in the sky, clouds move lazily with the breeze. It was as though she were seeing it for the first time.

"How long have you lived in Loveland?" he wondered. Surely, she would have come across this view sooner if it had been for very long.

"My whole life," she told him without looking away from the panorama.

Exiting the car, he held out a hand for her to take as she followed suit. Her movements were graceful as she walked with him. She was fluid, not toppling over in her heels. Popping the trunk of his car, he pulled out the basket and blanket his mom had given him before picking up Sophia.

The skirt of her dress blew around her knees with the wind as they walked to a small spot a few yards away from the car. "Hold this?" he asked her, handing over the basket as he spread the blanket out on the grass. Taking the carrier from her, he set it on the corner of the throw while taking each of his boots off and placing them on two other corners.

Satisfied, he looked up to see her watching him with a raised eyebrow. "So the wind doesn't blow it up," he explained.

"Makes sense," she whispered taking off her own shoes to sit on the blanket.

Christ.

Even sitting down, she was the picture of elegance. Ankles crossed and to the side of her body, her ruffled skirt covering her calves.

Taking off his coat, he sat behind her, curving his form around hers, boxing her in. "I'm gonna be honest here. Ma packed this picnic basket, and I'm a little afraid of what's inside." He loved his mother, but she could be a bit of a free spirit when needed, and that included doing crazy things when they least expected it.

"It can't be that bad," Soph said as she opened the lid on one side.

He watched as she began pulling dishes out.

Garlic and oyster linguini. Stuffed roasted red peppers. Chocolate covered strawberries, pears, and honey-glazed bananas for dessert. All aphrodisiacs. If he didn't love the crazy woman so much, he might be tempted to strangle her.

Sophia's gasp of surprise had his eyes widening as she pulled out a bottle of Moët & Chandon Dom

Pérignon his mother had been saving for a special occasion for years.

After inspecting the bottle, Sophia looked at him wide-eyed. "This is a very expensive bottle of champagne, Lennox. Why would she give this to us?"

He honestly didn't care about the bottle or what was in the basket, all he knew was that it showed his mother's affection for Soph, so he responded, "She must agree that you're something special." He watched, fascinated, as a blush stole its way up her delicate features.

Lennox had to be one of the sweetest and nicest people she'd ever met. His interest in her was unparalleled to anything she'd known before. The look in his gaze as he watched her pull the items from the carrier never wavered. He didn't pay attention to what she was grabbing; his sole focus was on her reaction to each one.

It didn't go unnoticed that Lorraine had packed a celebratory dinner full of carnal delights meant to seduce. To say she was shocked would be an understatement. She smiled, thinking of the kiss they'd shared earlier. The way she'd melted into his arms.

With him, she felt safe and loved. Two things she'd never known before. Two things she shouldn't count on in the future. Because if life had taught her anything, it's that she was unlovable and useless.

"Hey." His fingers on her chin drew her attention to the concentrated look on his face. "What's with the expression?"

Clearing any emotion from her face, she lied, "Nothing," with the fake smile she'd grown used to.

He seemed doubtful as he watched her but didn't push, for which she was grateful. She had so many issues, she wasn't even sure being on this date with him was a good idea.

They sat quietly eating, both lost in their own thoughts. Sophia wanted to fight every last one of her instincts to have a real, solid relationship with Lennox. She wanted to let go of the pain from her past. Her mother's words of discouragement and berating kept ringing in her ears, though.

A warm palm on her arm pulled her away from the painful words. "Calm down, Soph," he encouraged, his thumb rubbing circles on the inside of her elbow.

Twisting to face him, her skirt rode up her thigh an inch and his eyes flamed with want. "I don't know how to do this," she confessed, playing with the hem of her dress.

"I figured as much, darlin'," he said with a smile. No judgment, which amazed her. She was so used to everyone passing their own assessments around about her. Telling her when she was doing everything wrong, which was often.

"Oh," she murmured softly. Needing to get her head out of the negative space that seemed to consume her, she asked him, "How is Lorraine?" She had so much respect and love for the other woman, her attitude towards life was refreshing in a way she, herself, had never taken the time to discover.

"Ma's good." He smiled. "She was going to call you yesterday. Something about bridge, or cards, or something."

She had called. Sophia hadn't answered. She wasn't in the right frame of mind for speaking to her. She knew Lorraine would have picked up on what she was feeling. She would have drilled her on it, too.

"I, uh, missed her call." She looked away upon answering him.

"Such a contradiction," he told her. Eyes shooting to his, she didn't have to ask what he meant before he answered. "You're all sweet and soft one

78

minute." His fingers brushed along her cheek. "Then secrets and mystery the next. I never know what to expect with you."

Her face leaned into his palm at his words. "I'm sorry." She was. She didn't want to have secrets or tell him lies. The problem was, she didn't know what she wanted or even how to obtain it when she did.

"Don't need to be sorry, sweetheart. When you're ready, you'll tell me about the haunting I see in your eyes. You'll tell me what your dreams are."

"And if you get tired of waiting?" Sucking her bottom lip between her teeth, she waited with baited breath.

"I'll never tire, Sophia. I will be here." *How could he know?*

"You barely know me."

"I know enough."

How could she trust that? Everyone she should have been able to trust in her life had always let her down. It was never a matter of if, simply the question of when.

The look in his eyes showed her so much. Everything he felt, everything he wanted to feel. She quickly realized that while she was protecting her own heart, he was trying to protect his as well. Only he knew what love was, what it meant to get it, and he was attempting to make her see and understand, too.

"I want to–" she started to say when he interrupted.

"Then that's enough. If you want this, us, then I will fight enough for both of us. You just have to *want* it."

Wanting something for herself was such a foreign feeling. "The last time I wanted something I was six," Sophia told him, remembering Christmas that year and the one present she wanted. Only to have it taken from her in the blink of an eye.

"What was it?"

"It's silly," she replied, heat engulfing her cheeks as she thought about the toy now.

"Not if it was important to you." He made her believe that.

"There was this American Girl Doll, Kailey, she was new and so popular. I used to collect them. Well, I wanted one for Christmas that year." She smiled remembering the anticipation. "Daddy bought one for me." Her smile was genuine as she thought of his happiness that day, too. Until her mother. Always her mother.

"What happened?" Lennox asked her, sensing something went wrong.

Her smile faded. "My mother was so drunk already. Or maybe it was still from the night before. I have no idea. I didn't even get to open the box, and she'd ripped it from my hands and tossed it in the fire my father had started only minutes before."

"Christ," he muttered.

"Something like that," she agreed. "She was so angry that my father had given me the one and only toy I'd wanted. It was all I had asked for. She stumbled around the living room, cursing, calling me horrid names, and my father even worse ones. By the time she was done, she'd ripped everything down that resembled Christmas. We never really celebrated it again after that."

"You're mother's a real piece of work."

She couldn't argue with him there.

Listening to Soph explain what her mother was like when she was so fucking young left Nox feeling incredibly lucky for what he did have. Then, now, and the future. He'd known the love of a parent who wanted him. Whereas, she seemed to have one parent torn between loyalties and broken from love, while the other just hated her. He couldn't comprehend it.

He'd hoped she would open up during their date, get to know him so he could know her. With the sad look on her face, he knew he had to turn things around. Get her happy again.

"What's one thing you'd love to do?" he asked, not watching her. He could tell she felt like he put her under scrutiny when he did, so he watched as the wildflowers swayed with the breeze.

"Anything?" she asked, catching onto what he was doing. He nodded, and she continued. "I'd love to make a snowman."

The laughter in her voice had his head turning. "A snowman?" he repeated in disbelief. "You've never made one?"

"Nope."

Even though winter was over, he suddenly wished for a massive snow storm.

"We'll do something about that this year," he reassured her, silently making it his life's mission to give her the simplest things he could.

"What about you?" she asked him.

"I'd love to go to the Grand Prix in Spain."

"You've never been?" She gasped in mock horror.

"Don't get smart with me, woman." She tried holding in her laughter and failed. The tinkling sound was music to his ears. The lightness on her face was a sight to behold. The freedom in her eyes was his goal.

"Okay, okay, sorry." The damn girl was gasping for breath through her laughing. He couldn't be fucking happier than right in that moment.

"Do your brothers share your same love of cars?" she finally asked.

"No. Levi, he's a little more secretive. He likes cars well enough, but that boy has got things going on in his head no one knows about. Loch hasn't found what he's passionate about yet. He goes through the motions, pretending so he can fit in. I have a feeling he's likely to get himself in trouble trying to find what he wants to spend the rest of his life doing." It'd be easier, less stressful if Loch and Levi could just focus on the cars. But they never had the same interest as Nox did.

"Your mom said the same thing weeks ago," she told him.

"Really?" He perked up, "What else has Ma said?"

She cleared her throat before answering. "That you were lonely."

"She did, did she?" He was, he just hadn't thought he was obvious about it.

"Are you?" Soph hesitated in asking him.

Thinking about it, Nox knew he had to be honest. If he wanted her to give him everything she was, then he had to give her the same courtesy. Trouble was, he didn't know how to explain why. It's not as though he was hurting for having people around him. His brothers were always there, his Ma was constantly hounding him for one thing or another, and women flocked to him like birds. Whatever that meant. He just had no logical reason for being lonely when he was surrounded by everyone he loved daily.

Except...

He wanted a reason to go home to at night. A warm body to keep him company. Someone to share his day with.

Looking at Sophia, he saw all of those things with her and more.

"I am," he finally answered her. "I have everyone around me, but I'm missing someone to share it all with." He knew if he said he was missing her at his side, she'd get spooked. So he kept his mouth shut.

"I can understand that," she responded. In her eyes, he saw that she really did. Maybe more than he did. She had more money than anyone he knew, yet she had to be the loneliest person he'd ever met.

Cupping the back of her neck, he brought her closer to him. As their lips met, he told her, "We'll work on that, together," just as he claimed her mouth with his.

She hesitated at first, only taking what he offered, not giving anything herself. Until he nipped her lip, and she came alive.

Like a match to flame.

Thunder to lighting.

She exploded.

She soared as he explored her mouth. A blend of sweet champagne and spicy food. She was the perfect mix. When she moaned into his mouth, his other hand went to her thigh, rubbing softly up her satin-smooth skin with his fingertips as they kissed.

He didn't push for more than she was ready to give, and she didn't back away. They found a flawless harmony of give and take. Pulling his shirt over his head, a light touch on his chest alerted him to her soft, questioning contact. Her delicate fingers explored his hard muscles as his hand slid up her thigh, clutching her plump ass cheek and pulling her closer to him.

She smoothed her fingertips up his chest tentatively until she reached his jaw, cupping him the way he'd done so many times to her before. He groaned in delight as she rubbed her dainty digits through his stubble while she explored his features the way he wanted to explore her body.

Before long, they were laying side by side, eyes connected, fingers intertwined while the sun began to go down. When a shiver worked through her, he finally admitted it was time to take her home, no matter that he just wanted to lay there all night with her in his arms.

CHAPTER
FOUR

DISTANCE ISN'T AN ISSUE BECAUSE
IN THE END. I HAVE YOU.

THE DRIVE HOME was shrouded in intimate silence. Something Sophia never thought she'd experience. She'd read about those long, quiet silences in books, the ones filled with tension. A silence so deep neither time nor space could transcend the meaning of.

The silence of two people who could read the other like open books.

Familiar dread squeezed her heart and swallowed the happiness she'd been enjoying as they pulled up the driveway to her prison. She hated that house with every fiber of her being. It radiated with lies. Lies no one but the three people living there knew existed.

A curtain on the top floor of the east wing fluttered as Lennox turned the ignition off, and she just knew it was her mother. She could almost feel the animosity being shot at her.

"I had fun," Lennox said, pulling her from thoughts of what was to come.

Mentally shaking her head, she plastered a smile on her face, telling him, "It was really nice. Those wildflowers were beautiful, too."

"We could do it again," he suggested, taking her off guard.

"I think I would like that," she responded, smiling.

"Good. I'll be back day after tomorrow." The shock on her face was mirrored back at her as he climbed from the vehicle and she saw her reflection in the side window.

As he opened her door, she squeaked out, "So soon?"

"Can't let you think too hard about me not coming back, now can I." It wasn't a question. She *would* doubt he'd want to return after everything she'd told him.

"Is this... Are we...?" She didn't know how to ask.

"Dating?" he finished for her. Nodding her head, he told her, "No." Disappointment slammed her like a ton of bricks. "Dating is for kids. We're in a relationship, Sophia."

"Relationship." She repeated. "I thought that came after the dating?" She had no idea about any of those things. She was such a novice.

"For some, sure. I'm too old for that shit, Soph. I know what I want. And what I want, you're not ready for, so compromising is what I'll have to do."

"This is a compromise?"

"Yup." It was hard not to laugh at his smug smile.

Shrugging her shoulder, she would try and go with it. "Okay."

Walking up the steps to her front door with his hand on her back, she felt cherished. A feeling she could definitely get used to.

"Thursday, six o'clock, be ready, darlin'," he told her as he leaned down to give her a kiss on the cheek. His lips left an imprint as he pulled away.

"What will we do?" She wanted to know how she should dress. She loved wearing frilly dresses, but she had a feeling she wouldn't always be able to with him.

"Dinner and a movie, maybe," he answered. "Goodnight, sweet Sophia." He brought her hand to his mouth for one last kiss before opening the door for her to go inside. As it shut, she had the most amazing feeling of anticipation she'd ever felt before.

Never in her life had she looked forward to another day. Never had she wanted the night to end sooner than it did. Never had she wanted to stay out all night if only to keep the euphoric feeling.

All too soon everything came crashing down as her mother's footsteps and snarled words entered the room. "I told you to stay away from him!" She grimaced from behind Sophia's stance by the door.

Wishing she could dart through the huge oak doors, she turned and spat out, "You haven't been with him." She believed him on that.

"Oh, Sophia, so naïve. So dumb. When will you learn?" The false saccharine smile on her mother's face had Sophia wary of what the woman would do.

Taking a deep breath, she asked her mother, "Why do you hate me so much?"

Breath held, she waited for an answer.

The ugly look that crossed Rebecca's face wasn't what she had expected, nor were the words. "Because you ruined everything!" she yelled.

"How?" The word barely made it past her tight throat.

"Anthony wanted to be the perfect family; he wanted what he couldn't have. What I wouldn't give him. Stupid child, you are nothing." Sophia stood frozen as her mother ranted. "You should have been dead. You weren't supposed to be born. But the idiot couldn't keep it in his pants." *What was she saying?* "I made do the best I could with the fool I was given, but Lord help me, you are too stupid to function." That word again. "I wish he'd left you in the trash where he found you!"

"What?" she whispered in horror.

"Sophia!" Braxton's voice could be heard from...

The kitchen? she thought. She didn't know where he was. She didn't know anything.

The trash?

"I was garbage?" She was sure the pain vibrating through her could be heard in her voice.

"Sophia!" Braxton called again, closer that time. She still couldn't answer.

"That was after you were choked, of course." *How could she be so smug?*

"I don't understand." The words were more for herself, but her mother caught them.

"Of course, you don't. You're too damn stupid. You, Sophia, are the biggest mistake of my life. My ultimate failure. My regret. *Stupid Sophia*, always wanting to be loved. *Stupid Sophia*, always wanting what she can't have." She began walking closer as she sang about how dumb she was. "*Stupid Sophia*, always taking what's mine. And have no doubt, *Stupid Sophia*, Lennox Hogan is mine."

Her heart was beating out of control, her mind was running a million miles a minute. And yet, it all made sense. The hate, the contempt, every painful memory and word.

"I'm sorry," she murmured meekly. Hating how weak she sounded but unable to do anything about it.

"Rebecca!" Braxton's voice was full of warning as he saw them.

Leaning into Sophia, her mother whispered, "What do you say, should I take him for a ride, too? Make him hate you as much as I do? It worked with your father." Before the woman could say anything else, Brax had pulled her away.

But it was too late. The damage was done.

Her feet carried her up the stairs before he could say a word.

Laughter followed her, as did the cruel words.

Stupid Sophia.

Lennox felt like he was on cloud nine. The night with Sophia had gone far better than he could have imagined. He wasn't too enthusiastic about dropping her back off at home with the wicked witch there, but he had no choice in the matter.

Hearing about the way she'd been treated, he was amazed she was still so sweet and not bitter or jaded. There was a light in her that no matter how hard the older Bennett woman tried, couldn't be dimmed.

As he drove home, the night clear, moon high

and full in the sky, he knew exactly what he was going to do for their next date. The Fort Collins Museum of Discovery had an amazing observatory he thought she would thoroughly enjoy.

Soph was a woman of polish and prestige that enjoyed the littlest things, and that pleased him more than anything. While he was well off and his business was booming, he didn't think he could give her the things she was used to without tanking himself. And not having her in his life wasn't an option. Her smile and light were intoxicating. After the way she'd come apart in his arms earlier, he knew he was addicted. All the little aspects of her personality set her apart from any other woman he'd met or dated.

She'd asked him inquisitive questions about who he was as a person as well as what he wanted from life. Not many men or women cared about the fundamentals anymore.

Pulling up in front of his modest two story, four-bedroom house, he admired all the hard work he'd put into the structure. When he'd bought it, everything was in shambles. He was still renovating the basement, a bedroom, and one of the bathrooms.

The master suite was his pride and joy. He'd

spent the most time and money there, wanting it to be a perfect oasis for his partner when they finally connected. He'd wanted somewhere they could escape to when kids were down for the night.

The garage door went up as he moved closer to the entrance. Slowly pulling in and parking, he locked the garage up and entered the house through the mudroom door that doubled as a laundry room. Tossing his keys on the counter, he saw the light on the answering machine flashing. Pressing play as he passed, his annoyance spiked.

"Nox, baby, I miss you. Call me." The nasally voice belonged to a woman he'd been on a handful of dates with. She'd wanted more than he was offering after getting to know her.

Hitting delete, he made his way through the dining room and up the carpeted staircase, passing the first bedroom and guest bathroom as he did. The master suite was at the very back of the house, kept separate from the rest of the bedrooms. Shedding his coat, he tossed it on the lounge chair centered between the two big bay windows, next to the walk-in closet.

Sitting on the end of the bed, he undid his boots, kicking them to the side as he pulled his t-shirt over his head. Next went his jeans as he walked to the master bath. Intent on having a hot shower, he shucked off his boxer briefs as he leaned forward to turn the water on.

Hopping into the warm spray, he took a moment as he always did to admire the labor he'd put into the room. The glass-enclosed shower stall was in a corner so that he could see the entirety of the space. The huge clawfoot tub was under the Lucite crystal beveled window next to the shower. There was a vanity with a small bench seat between the his and hers sinks directly across from him. Everything gleamed with white marble. He'd wanted to leave most of the house as plain as possible, so when he did marry, his new bride would have a say in the décor.

Drying off, he stepped out onto the shag carpet, thinking about how well Sophia would look laying in the white tub, her long blonde hair hanging over the edge. Or her ass hanging off one of the sinks as he loved her body.

Walking back into his room, he could see her on his pillow as well. Body supple, waiting for him, hair fanned out on the white sheets. Yeah, that was an image he would most definitely like to see come true.

Striding to his dresser, he opened the top drawer to grab a pair of boxers, slipping them up his still drying legs. Taking his towel to the hamper, he grabbed the jeans he'd tossed in there, searching the pockets for his cell.

Climbing into bed, he decided to text Sophia. Tell her goodnight and how much he'd enjoyed their evening.

Nox: I had a great time tonight. Thanks for taking a chance ;)

Putting the phone down beside him, he didn't expect an immediate answer, so he grabbed the remote for the small TV sitting on top of his dresser. Turning it on, he flipped through channels until he found a hockey game. Sports weren't exactly his go to, but it'd do in a pinch when he was waiting to hear back from his girl.

His girl.

Something he was more than willing to get used to.

His phone finally chimed as he was thinking of just how quickly he could convince her to move in. Disappointment settled in his gut as he saw it was Levi.

Levi: Heard a few rumors about your girl...
Nox: Such as...?

Three bubbles popped up as his brother was typing.

Levi: One is that she's not even a real Bennett.

With the way her mother treated her, he wasn't shocked to hear that.

Levi: Another is that Tony had an affair.

Happened all the time.

Levi: Third is he wanted an heir, she wants the money and will do anything to ensure she gets it.

Levi: ANYTHING!

His mind was working overtime with the implications of the third rumor.

Nox: You think Rebecca could be behind the threats?

Levi: I wouldn't be shocked. That bitch has her claws into a few wealthy men. Makes me wonder what she sees in you ;)

Nox: Thanks for that. Let me know if you hear anything else.

Levi: Anytime bro.

Nox was reeling. It was hard to imagine a mother hating her child so much that she'd threaten her.

Fuck.

Now he was even more worried about her.

Nox: Sugar, you there?

He watched the phone as though she would magically start typing.

Nox: I'm worried about you. Please answer.

He wasn't above begging for what he needed from her. Especially about her health and well-being. He sat and stared, waiting for what felt like a lifetime before the little bubbles appeared that she was typing.

"Thank God," he muttered.

When her phone beeped, Sophia wasn't ashamed to admit she hid under her blankets. All she could think of was the threatening texts she'd gotten earlier. When it had gone off again, she chewed the nails off of one hand in record time. If her mother saw, she'd kill her.

It was the third chime that had her finally grabbing it and daring a quick look. Lennox's name flashed like a beacon across the screen. All the pain she'd been swamped with fell away as if it were never there. Seeing his messages, she was quick to answer.

Sophia: Sorry! I was getting ready for bed. I had a good time too.

He was quick to answer.

Lennox: Good. I look forward to the next one. I have plans in motion already!

Sophia: Care to tell me?

For the first time she could remember, she felt carefree. The feeling was addicting.

Lennox: It's a secret...

Sophia: Didn't your mama tell you secrets aren't nice? :p

Lennox: She told me only the best ones are ;)

Sophia: Ohhhh I wonder what it could be...

Lennox: LOL nice try sweet Sophia. Get some rest beautiful, and I'll see you soon.

Sophia: Goodnight Lennox.

Putting the phone on her night table, she pulled the blanket up around her chin, feeling warm instead of cold. Feelings of being wanted were so drastically different from what she normally felt that it was hard to come to terms with it.

As sleep tried to take her, she heard her parents fighting from down the hall again. She couldn't register the words exchanged, but the anger and hatred were just as telling. She could never understand why they were still together when they hated each other so much.

Pushing them from her mind, she latched onto

the way Lennox had made her feel coming apart in his embrace with only soft touches. The glow of his praise swept her off to see the sandman before long, and for the first time in years, she had a peaceful sleep.

CHAPTER
FIVE

BEAUTY BEGINS THE MOMENT YOU
DECIDE TO BE YOURSELF.

Only thirty-six more hours until Nox could see Soph again. He didn't like the time apart. Not seeing her and knowing for himself that she was okay was messing with his concentration once again.

Hearing the rumors Levi had told him made a sick sort of sense with the way she was treated at home. The idea to confront her father, at the very least, about it lingered in his mind. His only fear was the trouble it would cause for his girl.

He decided to send her a quick text before leaving for work for the day.

Nox: Good morning beautiful. Have a wonderful day, call me when you get up.

Slipping his phone into his pocket, he walked out to his car and was backed out of the drive and on the road in record time. He had appointments lined up all day, so he was hopeful to be kept busy until it was time to close shop.

Traffic was heavy for only six in the morning as he made his way downtown. Hitting every red light on the way made it feel even longer of a drive.

When he managed to get to the shop, he was shocked to see Levi's Charger parked out front already. His brother wasn't much for being early for anything, especially work.

Parking, he made his way around back where he

was sure the younger man would be. Unlocking the entrance gate for where parts get delivered, he was shocked to see Levi slumped over alongside the auto parts office door. His face a mix of black and blue, and his shirt was ripped at the collar.

"Shit, Levi." He rushed over to his brother. Shaking his shoulder, Levi swung as he was startled to consciousness. "What the hell!"

"Oh, Nox. Sorry." His voice was muffled by the fat lip he was sporting.

"What the hell happened?" Nox asked, gingerly helping his brother to his feet. Steadying him with a shoulder under his arm as he unlocked the door allowing them into the building.

"Some dick jumped me," he mumbled.

Nox wasn't buying it.

Levi had been off for a while now, and he was worried. He always had a bruise from something somewhere on his body, and every time he or Loch would ask about it, he'd shrug it off as nothing.

Nox wouldn't back off this time. He couldn't. Something was seriously wrong with the man, and he was determined to find out.

Stumbling into his office, he dropped his brother on the small couch with a groan as he landed. Going to the mini fridge in the corner, he grabbed a bottle of water. Tossing it to him, he went for the Tylenol he kept in the top drawer of his desk. Shaking three out, he handed them to Levi as he walked up to him.

Waiting as the man downed the medication, he crossed his arms leaning against his desk. "What is going on with you, Levi?"

His brother eyed him with the one he could open, assessing Nox like he was the one that kept coming to work bruised. "It's fine, Nox. Leave it alone."

"Are you fucking kidding me?" He exploded, arms thrown wide as he took a step towards his brother. "If I didn't know you so damn well, I'd think you were in some kind of trouble, but I know you're not that stupid. That Pop didn't raise you to be such an idiot. So I'll ask again, what's going on?"

Pain had flashed in the other man's eyes before he looked away. "I'm just not ready to tell, okay?"

He could hear it. Something was going on, and for whatever reason, it made him too nervous to share with Nox.

"Fine. But Levi," he waited for him to look into his eyes, "I'm here. Just because we're blood doesn't mean we ain't friends. I won't judge."

Levi nodded in relief. "Thanks, bro."

"Not me you gotta worry about. It's Ma when she

finds out." He laughed, walking out of the room as Levi cringed thinking about the reign of terror their pint-sized mother would bestow upon him the first time she saw him all bruised up.

Dismissing his brother's beating, Lennox got to work on the engine of one of the sweetest sixty-six Chevelles he'd ever laid eyes on. The owner had been restoring it for years, and Nox finally got to put the engine together and, hopefully, hear the beautiful rumble by the end of the week.

Going to his work station, he put some classic rock on the radio to listen to as he began reading the original engine manual. Double checking parts as he went, not wanting to have to take anything apart once he'd started.

As his mind was quickly consumed with the task at hand, and the music pumped through his blood, he never felt the phone vibrate in his pocket.

Sophia sat in her father's empty office, waiting for the man to show up. She felt like he was avoiding her because when she'd called to him as he was walking out the door, he'd stopped for a second before continuing on his way.

His pause baffled her.

Everything was confusing her.

There were more bodyguards around the house than when she went to bed the night before. Had the threat gotten worse? Was it no longer just about her? And what about the things her mother had said when Lennox had dropped her off after their date. Was it true?

She had so many questions, and nobody seemed to want to answer her.

"Sophia." Braxton's voice from the door drew her back from her thoughts. "You shouldn't be in here."

Her eyes narrowed on him as he held the door open for her, obviously thinking she'd leave. "No. I should be in here. Everyone keeps acting like I'm some fragile little pixie and not telling me a damn thing! I won't leave until I have answers. And since this is the only place my father will step foot in within the house, I'll either wait here or leave and never come back."

His bark of laughter at her threat was insulting. "Where are you going to go, Soph? Do you have a friend that would let you stay for free with no job and no skills? What exactly are you going to do?"

His words punctured a hole into her heart.

"Don't be stupid, Sophia. You can't leave. It's not safe out there for you." Braxton continued on.

There it was. Even someone she considered as a new friend thought her stupid.

She was so tired of feeling like nothing and nobody to everyone around her. She was never treated as an equal. Barely tolerated as a human being.

Standing up, she smoothed the skirt of her pleated dress against her thighs before walking forward. She wouldn't meet his eyes, refused to let him know the words he'd spewed had hit their mark.

Stopping after she'd walked past him, she said, "If I'm such a nobody, why are you here?" She didn't care if he responded or not. She left.

Going up to her bedroom, Sophia switched out her pumps for the Chucks she'd bought forever ago, grabbed a jacket because the sun wasn't out, and her purse. Quietly walking down the staircase, she heard voices from her father's office as she passed. She stopped only long enough to make sure that Braxton was in there with the man and to be sure the coast was clear.

Leaving through the massive front doors that always seemed more pompous than welcoming, she walked on down the driveway and to the street.

Pulling her phone from her purse, she searched for Lennox's body shop, hoping she wasn't being too forward by showing up unannounced. Deciding she'd send him a quick message, she saw that he'd sent her one early that morning.

Sophia: Good morning. I have to come downtown today, was hoping I could stop by?

Putting the phone back, she resumed her trek. With nearly twenty miles to walk, she knew she would either have to hail a cab or catch a bus, eventually. While not out of shape, she certainly wasn't prepared to walk such a far distance.

The cloud-covered sky and cool breeze made her decision quicker than she anticipated. Shivers racked her body as she walked until finding a bus stop. With a quick search on her phone, she found the next bus would come in eight minutes.

Lucky timing on her part.

Searching through her wallet, she found the right amount of change. Now she just hoped she wouldn't get lost when it came time to switch buses. The wait was nearly torturous as it seemed like time stood still and the wind picked up, making the small bus shelter basically ineffective.

Her cell phone chimed in her purse just as the bus made its appearance. Once on and her fare paid, she sat in the first available seat, hoping she didn't sit in gum or something else. Pulling her phone out, Braxton's name flashed across the screen as a missed call and two texts. She debated even opening them, not wanting to speak to him after his harsh treatment of her.

As she put the phone back, all those TV drama shows passed through her mind about tracking through cell phones. Quickly making a decision, she shut her phone down, hating that if Lennox did call or text her back, she would miss it.

Hopefully, she would be with him soon, if she didn't get lost first.

The bus was mostly empty, only a few young kids sitting at the back talking. Being on it, she realized just how sheltered she was. It was quite literally the first time she'd taken public transportation.

It wasn't horrible, but the smell of stale sweat made it not so great either. Watching as the neighborhoods passed by, going from her upper-class community into what she thought would be the working class was depressing. Seeing her nice clean streets turn into these cracked, pothole-filled ones made her sad.

What made rich people so special that they got an entirely new road when potholes occurred? Why did they deserve all the finer things? She'd bet her bottom dollar that the families living in these homes paid more in taxes than hers did. She hated that there was even a difference in society.

Before her mind could get too lost, the bus pulled into the depot where she was to catch her next one. Stepping off the vehicle, she searched the signs for the number of her connection.

Men watched her as she walked, almost like they knew she didn't belong there. That she was too rich to be taking public transit. Technically, she wasn't rich, her parents were. Sophia didn't have a dime to her name other than the trust fund her Aunt Millie had left her, and she couldn't touch that until she was twenty-five.

Seeing the sign with her next bus number on it, she took shelter in the small structure just behind it, sitting next to a young woman with a small child of about five. They were huddled in coats that had to be two sizes too big.

"Hi," the little girl whispered once she was settled.

Looking down to the crystal clear blue eyes staring at her, she smiled. "Hi." Sophia's voice just as quiet.

"You have pretty hair like Cinderella." Her voice was full of wonder.

Smiling bigger. "Thank you. I always liked her." Sophia looked up to the mother, wanting to make sure she wasn't upset by her child speaking to a stranger. The other woman smiled softly with an encouraging nod. "Do you have a favorite princess?" Sophia asked the girl.

She thought about it for a minute before answering. "I really like Belle. She's not a real princess, but she sure is nice."

"You know, I think being a princess is more about being kind to others than having a title," she told the girl.

"I like that." The child grinned as a bus pulled up. Seeing it wasn't hers, Sophia continued to wait as the pair got up to leave. "Goodbye." The girl waved.

"See you, princess." She winked at the little one's surprised face.

Some things never ceased to amaze her as their bus left. One short conversation about princesses with a small girl, and she felt her mood lift. The pain and hurt from that morning still lingered but not as deeply. She didn't feel suffocated by the hateful words anymore.

She still didn't want to go back, though. Going

back would mean losing another piece of herself. Going back would mean facing people who cared nothing about her. As her bus pulled up, she didn't know what she was going to do, just that she needed a new perspective.

———

As "Human" by Rag'n'Bone Man blasted from the speakers on his radio, Nox continued to work on the sweet ride under his hands. He was fitting the dynamics of the engine in and replacing corroded wires when Mac, one of his newest hires, called out to him. "Yo, Nox! You got a visitor."

"Who?" he called back, not looking up from the line he was trying to disconnect.

"Some sweet ride," was all he said, walking away.

Mac was a man of few words, only speaking when necessary. At times, it annoyed the hell out of him, others he enjoyed the quiet.

Giving up on the line, he grabbed the cloth off the fender of the car, wiping his hands as he walked to the front office. Not seeing anyone, he looked to Mac with a questioning brow.

"Your office. She don't belong out here."

Which had him more confused.

Knocking on his office door so whoever it was didn't startle, he walked in to see Soph. A huge smile lit his face at her presence.

"Soph? What are you doing here?" he asked walking over to her.

She turned to look at him, and he was bowled over with the dead emotion present in her gaze. "Hi," she whispered, tears gathering on her lids.

"Soph?" Before he could say anything else, she seemed to transform before him. Her stance stronger, the tears gone, and her eyes no longer desolate. He wondered for a brief moment if it had even been there.

"I, uh," she cleared her parched throat, "I hope it's okay I came. I sent a message earlier but had to shut my phone off, so I don't even know if you got it or not." She was nervous and rambling.

"Damn girl, calm down," he told her, leading her to the sofa Levi had finally left sometime while he was working.

"Sorry." She murmured.

"I didn't get your message, I've been rebuilding an engine all morning," he explained.

A forlorn expression crossed her face as she answered. "I should go then. I don't want to disturb you." As she stood, he got a look at her. She was a hot mess. Her beautiful little dress did not match the chucks on her feet, and her legs were bright red as if...

"Did you walk here?" he asked, shocked. Grabbing her hand, he yanked her back down to the sofa.

She wouldn't meet his eyes as she answered. "Well, sort of. I walked then took two buses, then walked again."

He was baffled. "Where's Braxton?"

She shrugged, still refusing to meet his eyes.

"Sophia," he snapped. He wasn't immune to the pain that still lingered in the depths of her gaze when she met his steely one. "What happened?" Something had to have. Braxton was supposed to be on her like glue when she was anywhere.

"Nothing," she murmured, playing with her skirt.

"Christ, woman," he growled pulling her into his arms, laying a light kiss on her head as she gripped his shirt. "Come on," he told her, standing. "You'll come work with me. You got a hair tie?" She dug through her purse and found one, whipping her hair up quickly. "Leave your stuff in here, I'll lock the door." She followed him out.

If he couldn't get her to talk about what happened and why she was acting more skittish than normal, then he would keep her by his side.

As they passed Mac at the front desk, the man raised his brows at her appearance. "Grab me the smallest set of coveralls you can find," Nox told him as they entered the shop.

"Wow," she cooed. When he looked back at her, he saw her gaze riveted to the car and engine he was fixing up.

"You know what that is?" he asked her. She shook her head no. "A sixty-six Chevelle. Mint condition, all original parts. Seats were just reupholstered to their original glory." He was shocked at how riveted she was to what he was saying. He didn't figure her for having an interest in cars.

"And you're building an engine?"

"Yes and no. It's the same engine, I'm just modifying it. Replacing a few old parts with new ones. It's still the original V-8 as when the owner bought it." He smiled, hoping not to have confused her too much.

"Here ya go, boss." Mac interrupted them, handing him the coveralls.

"Thanks, Mac." The man lingered as Nox led Soph to the bathroom to put them on. "Slide these over that pretty dress," he said. As she closed the door behind her, he turned around to see the young mechanic still standing there. "Something I can help you with, Mac?" he asked, a bite in his tone.

"Uh," he seemed to be dumbstruck before shaking the cobwebs from his brain, "Who is she?"

Nox didn't hesitate in answering. "My girl. She comes in here, no one messes with her."

"You got it, boss," he agreed, walking away.

Some of his guys were real dicks. Soph was pin-up perfection as far as he was concerned. Her light hair, innocent aura, and flared dresses were perfect drooling material for them all. Thank God, she hadn't worn her typical pumps coming in, or he didn't think Mac would have been nearly as gentle-manly as he'd seemed.

"I guess my chucks match this, at least." Sophia's laughter had him turning around.

"I'd like to see it with the pumps, still." He winked, she blushed. "Come here, sweet girl." His arms were held wide for her.

She drifted into him. Effortless. Like they were meant to be in each other's arms. Her deep inhale as she rubbed her nose into his neck went to his head a little. Knowing she was trying to imprint his scent on her synapses was intoxicating.

Pulling back reluctantly, he led her by the hand to the bench with his tools and the engine. Grabbing her hips, he lifted her to sit on a cleared spot beside the engine.

"Damn do you look stunning," he muttered.

Seeing her prim and proper next to his dirty tools and a broken engine, the way her milky skin shined, was a massive turn on.

The look in Lennox's gaze was predatory. His fists clenched at his sides.

"Lennox?" she whimpered.

He didn't answer her, instead walking forward and capturing her mouth in a soul-defining kiss. The intensity rolling off of him in waves made her shiver in response as she tried to work her mouth with his.

He didn't let her. He easily took all control of the act. Devouring every last inch of her while smoothing his hands up her back to grip the ends of her thick hair, he pulled her head back, exposing the length of her throat. His entire mouth landed wide over her pulse, sucking to the point she knew he was going to leave a mark.

"Lennox," she moaned, squirming in his tight embrace.

"Damn, we got our very own pin-up girl." A

man's voice broke the moment. Embarrassment seared her cheeks in flaming red.

A deep growl left Lennox as he turned, blocking her from the other person's view. "Watch your fucking mouth, Joey," he snapped. So much anger in his tone.

A pregnant silence ensued.

"Girls don't belong here," the man, Joey, barked back.

She was feeling uncomfortable as Lennox stepped forward, getting into the guy's face. Before he said anything, one of his brothers, Lochlan, she thought, showed up, "Yo, Nox, what's going on?" he tried to ask diplomatically.

"Just Joey being a dick again."

"You forget who signs your paycheck, Joey?" Lochlan asked, still trying to keep Lennox from knocking him on his ass.

"Whatever." The man stormed off.

"Sophia, happy to see you," Lochlan greeted, walking to her.

"Hi," she whispered, her heart still in her throat.

Leaning closer, he whispered to her, "Keep him in line, will you?" Kissing her cheek, he walked off.

A soft hand wiping her cheek followed by a set of

lips had her eyes widening at the bold move. "What was that for?" she asked Lennox.

"Don't need his lips on you," he mumbled, walking over to the hood of the car he was working on.

She had to stifle her laughter at the possessive move.

Watching as he worked, she got to admire his methodical mind as he expertly and precisely put the car together. She had no idea what any of the parts were called, nor what they did, but she understood that each piece was like a puzzle. Needing to fit perfectly into certain spots or nothing would look right.

Legs crossed, leaning back, her eyes searched the rest of the building they were in. Cars, some half-built, some in stages of dismantling, and others complete, were in three rows, and for the first time, she wondered about his marketing.

She'd always enjoyed creating eye-catching flyers for school fundraisers. A picture was already forming in her mind about how to show the business aspect of his shop.

Stupid Sophia.

The images quickly died as the most haunted phrase of all time bit her in the ass. She knew it was dumb. He was obviously very successful if the shop's fullness was any indication.

The need to be a useful person in society was riding her hard, though. She was desperate not to go back home. She would do almost anything to stay away.

"Soph?" Lennox's voice pierced her out of control thoughts.

"Yes?" She put a smile on so he wouldn't guess where her mind had been at.

"You wanna tell me what's been going on with you?"

Shaking her head, she contradicted herself by speaking anyways. "Braxton and I got into a fight this morning."

Wiping his hands, he walked over to her. "About what?"

Quietly she answered, "My uselessness and stupidity as a person." Shame shook her entire body.

"Say what, now?" He sounded confused.

Closing her eyes, she said louder, "My uselessness and stupidity."

He was silent for so long, she began to worry that maybe he agreed with everyone else.

"I should go." Her words were quiet as she slipped off the bench she was sitting on. He made no move to stop her as she went through the door they'd entered. Chancing a glance back at him, he was still in the same spot.

As she walked into the front office, Mac and Joey were standing there as her tears threatened to spill. Mac smiled at her. Joey sneered, "He done with you already?"

Her gasp was audible as Mac shot Joey a dirty look.

Stupid.

Useless.

Whore.

She was nothing.

Rushing out the front door, she wasn't paying attention as a car skidded into the parking lot and clipped her as they came to a stop. Hands on the hood, the breath stolen from her body, she eyed the man behind the wheel with a wild stare as he climbed free of the vehicle.

"I am so fucking sorry. Are you okay?"

"I'm fine," she croaked, straightening up and walking away.

She was ready to be done with people. She was tired of being hurt and used. Being no one was exhausting.

It wasn't until she was four blocks away that she

realized she didn't have her purse, her phone, no money. She was stranded. With her mind in complete and utter chaos, she hadn't thought about them once she'd walked into the office and Joey had made his degrading remark.

Searching around her, Sophia had no idea where she was. She hadn't been paying attention while moving as far away from Lennox as she could. Church bells ringing from close by had her hustling in that direction. A block and a half later and she was standing in front of St. Catherine's Cathedral. The sheer size of the building intimidating as she walked up the steps to the large oak doors.

Opening them, she made her way inside quietly. Candles cast an ethereal glow around the large room as she was awestruck by the beautiful stained glass windows around the tops of the walls. The sun radiating through made a multitude of colors bounce off the sparkling surfaces.

A fountain of holy water was to her right as she entered mass. Stopping to dip her fingers, she made the sign of the cross and said a Hail Mary before continuing to sit in the last row of pews closest to her.

There were very few people inside the holy building as she sat for what could have been hours when another man came to sit in front of her. He was quiet while she thought about her situation, what she would do, where she would go.

Laying her head on the back of the bench in front of her, she had no answers. Nothing forthcoming. All she wanted was to have an ordinary life. Being in danger from whatever ghosts her father was seeing, wasn't going to help any.

"Please give me insight, help me understand," she whispered so quietly she didn't think anyone would hear.

"God is a mystery sometimes," the man said. "Sometimes he'll make you wait for his guidance. Sometimes his answers are right in front of you."

Her head popped up when he started talking. As he turned to look at her, she was shocked to see the white collar around his neck. She hadn't expected to see or speak to anyone, let alone the minister of the church.

His bright blue eyes met hers. "Sometimes we aren't ready for the answers we often seek." As he smiled, his eyes crinkled at the corners, and the candlelight shone off the gray hairs nearing his temple, giving him a distinguished look. "Are you alright, young lady?"

"Yes," she answered quietly. "Just trying to understand."

"Perhaps I can help?"

A sad smile crossed her face as she replied, "I don't think anyone can." She got up to leave. No destination in mind.

Uselessness.

Stupidity.

The words kept ringing in his head. When she'd spoken them, he'd been flabbergasted. Completely thrown off guard. He didn't understand how anyone could say something like that to another person, especially someone as sweet as Sophia.

"Nox!" Mac yelled from the door. It took him a moment to realize she was gone, and he was standing there like an idiot.

"What?" he snapped, walking over to the man.

"She's gone, dude."

His words froze Nox's heart. She couldn't be gone.

"Where'd she go?"

"Took off out the front after Joey was a dick, almost got hit by a car."

"You let her leave?" he bellowed.

Raising his hands, the man backed up two steps before darting a look at the waiting customer. "She took off east on Fifth Street," the customer answered him.

"You hit her?" Nox snarled.

"Whoa, no man. She came busting out the door like her ass was on fire and ran into the hood of my car. She walked off just fine."

Lennox wasn't listening as he ran out the door, hoping to find her, knowing he wouldn't.

"I can't believe I fucking hesitated," he snapped at himself. He was going to kill Braxton when he got ahold of the man. Making her believe whatever cruel things he'd said.

Going back into his office, he searched her purse until he found her phone. Turning it on, he prayed it wasn't password protected.

As the screen lit up, it started chiming with missed calls, texts, and voicemails as he swiped across the screen. Relief swamped him when it didn't ask for a passcode. Seeing the angry texts from Braxton telling her to stop being a spoiled brat boiled his blood. Once he found Soph, he'd deal with whatever the other man had done to make her so upset that she'd essentially run away from home.

127

Going through her contacts, he didn't see more than a dozen numbers. His, his mother's, Braxton's, her parents', and a few businesses'. Nothing personal. No friends or other family members. Nada.

He knew she was sheltered, kept to herself, but he hadn't thought it was quite that lonely. Seeing the evidence of it, he was a little sad for her. She had no one to go to when she needed a break from her home life.

A quick decision had him entering Lochlan and Levi's numbers just in case she needed an escape and couldn't get a hold of him.

Putting her phone back in her purse, he heard a car come screeching into the parking lot moments before the front door jingled. Walking into the reception area, he saw Braxton entering, his eyes narrowed as they landed on Nox.

"Where is she?" the man growled.

As he was about to answer, Rebecca walked in.

"Nope," his eyes bore holes through her, "get out."

"Excuse me?" Her fake innocence didn't fool him.

"You are banned from my property. Get. Out," he spoke through gritted teeth.

"I'm a paying customer!" Her outrage was unnecessary.

"Not anymore you're not. You have no open business with us. Now get out before I have you arrested for trespassing." He threatened.

"You wouldn't!" She gasped.

Mac picked up the phone, a smirk on his face. He'd never been fond of the older woman either.

"You'll regret this," she shouted, walking out.

"Pretty sure I won't," he commented to her retreating back. Turning his attention back to Braxton. "What do you want?" he feigned a bored tone. Even if Soph hadn't run off, he wouldn't give her up.

"Where's Sophia?" he asked again.

Shrugging his shoulder, he told the man, "Out." Not caring that he was, in essence, lying even though it was sort of true.

He could see as Braxton processed his lack of a real answer and surveyed his shop before he spoke. "I'll wait."

When he went to sit, Nox confronted him. "Why?" he asked, crossing his arms over his chest.

"Why what?" Braxton matched his stance.

"Why'd you say those things to her? You obviously know and have seen what goes on in that house, and yet you did it anyway. When we first met, you seemed to actually give a shit about her. Is that because she was a good little girl and did what you said?" His eyes narrowed to slits. "Or did you expect her to jump into your bed? When she didn't do that, you decided to show your real colors?"

There was a flash of emotion in the other man's eyes at Nox's words before he quickly masked it. "Mind your fucking business, Hogan, you have no idea what's going on."

Curling his upper lip in disgust with the so-called bodyguard, he said, "I know enough that the chances are it's her fucking mother that has her in danger and not her father. I know enough to know that neither of those people gives a shit about her, and you're only there for looks."

Taking a step closer to Nox, his voice was filled with menace. "You're pushing it, boy."

"No. I'm right on the fucking money. Now get the hell out of my shop before I have you thrown out. Soph won't be going back." He vowed. She wouldn't. Her home was toxic, and he was pissed at himself for allowing her to stay to begin with.

Braxton was torn, he could see it in the man's eyes. They were waging war with what he was paid to do, and what the right thing to do would be.

While Nox had no doubt the bodyguard cared

about Sophia, he doubted the man knew how to actually show it. He'd spent a good chunk of his adolescence around people like Braxton. Closed-off. War-torn. Fighting to free themselves from the gilded cages in their minds.

He refused to let Sophia be a causality of the man's inadequacies.

If only Nox could find her. Figure out why she took off.

He knew that she misunderstood his quietness, and that was on him. He had every plan to grovel, to tell her he'd been so shocked he couldn't comprehend what she was saying until it was too late.

CHAPTER
SIX

LOVE IS WHEN THE OTHER PERSON'S
HAPPINESS IS MORE IMPORTANT
THAN YOUR OWN.

THE COOL BREEZE had Sophia shivering as she sat on the front steps leading into the church. She'd figured out that she was quick to jump the gun when she'd run from Lennox. A fact she was regretting the colder it got.

It felt like her emotions were controlling her every thought and move. Whenever Sophia felt like she was getting a handle on someone, her common sense went out the window. While she contemplated how she was going to get home, she heard it. The svelte rumble of a familiar engine she'd only been acquainted with one time.

As the red beauty rolled around the corner, she watched as he searched the street slowly passing any place she could be hiding. When he came to a stop in front of the church, he didn't notice her at first. She could see the wildness in his gaze, the messy tousle of his hair like he'd been pulling on it. Stress lined his mouth with a frown as he looked in every direction.

As their eyes finally collided, she saw a multitude of emotions work through him. Relief that she was safe. Anger that she'd run. Happiness that she hadn't exactly left.

His door opened without a sound as he exited the beautiful machine. His steps were purposeful as he walked towards her. His gaze intent as he searched her for injuries.

"I'm sorry," she whispered when he was close enough to hear her.

Sitting beside her, he didn't hesitate in gripping her small hand in his calloused one. "Me, too."

"I shouldn't have left."

"You shouldn't have." He agreed.

"I wish I knew why I am the way I am," she admitted. Having never said it out loud before, she did wish she knew why her emotions were always so close to the surface. She wished she understood why she couldn't let someone in without having so much overwhelming doubt that she was often left hurt more from her own actions than theirs.

"Soph." The single word was full of so much emotion. "There's nothing wrong with you."

Her head swiveled to find him watching her carefully as she processed his words. "Of course, there is. How can there not be? I'm so overly emotional I think I'm stunted. I'm sure there's a word or phrase or something for it, but I don't know it because I'm just too dumb." Her heart rate was skyrocketing as she stressed over it.

"Sophia," he responded. This time he was full of rage. She could see the way his pulse flickered in his neck, the way his brows furrowed, and he clenched his free hand. "You aren't fucking stupid. You have to stop thinking that."

Not wanting to anger him further, she thought her words through carefully before answering. "I don't know how to be anything else."

"Christ, sugar." He sounded so frustrated. "She really fucked you up."

And what was she supposed to say to that? The *she* was clearly her mother.

She didn't have an answer for him. How could she deny it when she was so irrevocably screwed around in the head she didn't know how to defend it.

Standing, she honestly thought he was giving up with her. She wouldn't blame him, either. She was contradiction after contradiction and not necessarily in a good way.

"Let's go home, Soph." His words shocked her.

"Home?" she questioned, unable to hide the fear in her voice.

"Mine," was the only answer he gave.

Following along behind him, she hoped he wouldn't give up on her. She knew she was a hot mess but couldn't help it. It wasn't like she could just erase nineteen years worth of degrading remarks. Much as she'd like to.

The cool leather of the seats soaked through the coveralls she was still wearing as they left the church. She didn't pay attention during the drive, yet again, until fifteen minutes later when they pulled into the picture of every middle-class American home.

She felt him watching her as she ate up every small and large feature of his house. She knew he thought she would be upset or disgusted by the modesty of it, but it couldn't be further from the truth. It was a perfect two story structure. Not so big you couldn't find someone, not so small that you would run over each other while going from room to room.

As she watched the door lift, he slowly rolled the vehicle into the open space. The garage was undeniably his baby. It was like a lover for his car. All the tools and materials he would need to make just this one vehicle to his every specification were organized here. Or so she assumed as she knew nothing about cars.

"I know it's no mansion," he said as the car shut off.

Without looking at him, she replied honestly. "It's better." Climbing from the car, she walked to the door leading into the house. As he unlocked it, she preceded him, with his hand on her back, into a large mud room filled to the brim with more jackets than she was sure he needed.

Smiling over her shoulder at him, he had a sheepish look on his face. "Let's get you out of these, shall we?" He helped her slip free of the coveralls.

Guiding her through more of his home, she was delighted to see so many personal touches throughout while also keeping it sort of...plain. Untouched almost. Like he was waiting for a woman's flair.

Nox was trying to see his house through her eyes as she inspected the pictures he'd hung or the few knickknacks he had on shelves. What he saw was kind of sad.

A home without the warmth.

His plan had always been to have the home and let his woman do her thing when she moved in. Now, he almost wished he'd put some sort of personal touches other than pictures.

She didn't comment, though, and he knew she wouldn't. His Soph was too polite to tell him he needed color to brighten things up. That his enormous TV wasn't needed.

"Have you lived here long?" she asked, and he couldn't help laughing at her question.

Pulling her into his embrace, he kissed her lightly, answering, "A few years. It's a bachelor pad, isn't it?"

Her hands smoothing along his sides were more erotic than she probably intended. "A little bit."

Leading her to a stool at the breakfast nook, he pulled them each a bottled water from the fridge. Twisting the cap off hers, he handed it to her.

Both were quiet as they processed their thoughts. He knew he had to tell her about her mother and Braxton showing up, but honestly, he didn't want the spark in her eyes dimmed more than it had been.

"Your mother and Braxton showed up," he finally spat out.

"Oh." She stared at him expectantly.

"I banned your mom from the shop."

Shock had her mouth forming the perfect 'O' as she said, "She must have loved that."

"I think it's the first time anyone has ever made her *do* anything." He smiled, remembering Rebecca's shock.

"What did Braxton say?" She sounded worried.

"Before or after I accused him of wanting to sleep with you?" He smirked. Nox had no doubt any man with eyes wanted between her legs. Her innocence combined with her beauty would have any male drooling. Hell, he had been for days.

"He does not," she scoffed. Sophia really had no idea of her attractiveness which made her all that more alluring.

"Yeah, gorgeous, he does. Aside from that, I think he's remorseful for the things he said to you, and as much as it galls me to say, I do believe he cares about you."

"He has a funny way of showing it," she mumbled into her water.

"Which brings us back to what exactly happened today, Soph?" There was more going on than the argument she'd had with Braxton.

"It's stupid." She shrugged it off.

"I hate that you think you or anything involving you is stupid. Soph, something upset you. Talk to me," he demanded.

Sighing, her eyes darted around the room before coming back to land on him as she picked at the label on the bottle. "Dad's been avoiding me. So I was waiting in his office this morning. Braxton caught me." Nox watched as she took a few fortifying breaths. "When you dropped me off last night, she was on me." Soph didn't have to explain who *she* was. "She said some things. Really nasty things, and it made me wonder. I had questions only he could answer. Except, when I called out to him this morning, he ignored me. Which isn't normally like him. I know he's cold and aloof, but with me, he's always had a soft spot. Though, the past few years, he's grown colder. Which makes me wonder if my mother's claims are true. Maybe I am just that unlovable and useless." The last few words were spoken so quietly and with so much hurt that his own heart constricted.

Walking around the bar to her, he pulled her into his arms again. "You're not, Soph. I wish I could make you see you the way I do, the way Ma does." Rocking her in his arms, for the first time in his life, he felt helpless. Someone was after her, and yet, he couldn't help there. Her mother insulted and demeaned her every chance she got, and he still couldn't help with that, either.

"It's fine." She sniffed into his chest. It really wasn't fine. They were anything but fine.

Wanting to get her mind, and his, off her depressing home life, he asked, "Want something to eat? I can't promise much, but I'm sure I can scrounge up something." He pulled away to gaze down at her.

"Yes, please." Her voice was like cracked glass. Still pretty but slightly broken.

Walking to his fridge, he opened it and realized he had pretty much nothing of substance. "I need to shop more," he muttered. "The choices are eggs and cheese or cheese and eggs?" He flicked a smile over his shoulder to see her watching him.

"I'm allergic to eggs."

Color him shocked. "Seriously?"

Red tinged her cheeks. "Yes."

"Okay then, how about pizza?"

Her nose had wrinkled before she answered. "Not a fan."

His jaw dropped open. "You're shittin' me?" She shook her head. *Well, balls.* "Why not?"

Shrugging, she told him, "I'm not a fan of feta cheese, and that's all the cook would use at home. Something about it not being real pizza without it."

He couldn't help the laugh that exploded from him.

"Oh baby, have no fear, I'll take care of you."

"If you say so." She side-eyed him while he ordered the deep dish he liked.

Hanging up, he told her, "Half cheese, half

pepperoni and bacon. I'll make a pizza lover out of you yet." She gave him a disarming smile, full of indulgence. "Come with me, we'll get you something more comfortable to wear." He held out a hand for her to take. His idea being completely selfish. He only wanted to see her in his clothes.

They sat, they ate pizza, they laughed. Lord did he make Sophia laugh. She couldn't remember the last time if ever, she'd spent an evening relaxing with someone just for the sake of kinship. Lennox understood her in ways she didn't understand herself.

As the sun set and the clock chimed eleven p.m., she knew she couldn't keep him up any longer to avoid her nightmares.

"If you show me where the linens are, I can make a bed on the sofa?" she asked him shyly, not wanting to intrude.

A look entered his eyes she couldn't decipher as he grabbed her hand, making her choose between following him or losing the limb. He led her up the stairs, past the bedrooms, and into his room. She stood dumbfounded in the doorway.

When he started peeling his clothes from his

body, she was torn between wanting to see the rippling flesh underneath the straining Henley he wore and her modesty. Modesty won as she saw him unbuckling his jeans. Her eyes slammed shut, and her head turned away, his chuckle meeting her ears.

"What's so funny?"

It took a moment for him to answer. "You," his voice was soft in her ear, "trying not to look." His voice...like smooth velvet.

"I...I didn't want to overstep." Did she have to sound so naïve?

She felt the warmth of his hands seep through the shirt and shorts he'd given her to wear earlier as he encircled her waist. The hold was intimate, sensual, as he pressed her entire body against his own. There wasn't a single inch of space between them as they swayed back and forth. He didn't push for more than what she was giving, but he didn't back off either. She had a feeling he wouldn't.

"What," she had to clear her throat to get her question out, "what are you doing, Lennox?" Was that her voice? Soft and sexy.

"I love the way you purr my name, sweet Sophia." His murmured words did something to her. They were full of heat and a deep-seated need she didn't understand.

His hands began roaming her body, heating her from the outside into her core. Her body felt light-weight, her mind was heady with erotic thoughts as his lips slowly kissed along her neck.

Spinning her in his arms, their mouths crashed together like fuses. His grip on her hips was harsh as he dominated every thought in her mind. Her body came alive for him, her breasts felt heavy with the need to be touched while her sex pulsed with a desire to be worshipped. It was startling to realize she wanted all these sexual things she'd never even thought of before. As the back of her legs met the mattress and she stumbled, he pulled her further into his body, as if the mere thought of losing any contact with her was abysmal.

When his hands roamed further down her body, she lit up. Gone was any hesitation. In its place were complete obedience and a passion so intense she almost couldn't breathe. Her leg hitched onto his hip of its own volition while she tried to attach her body to his. With his hands on her ass, he started rocking her back and forth on his thigh, the friction against her core enough to send so much pleasure coursing through her body that she saw stars behind her lids.

Before she knew what was happening, her body exploded into an array of fireworks. She was tense yet limp. Hot but shivering. Her cries of rapture were captured by his lips as he slowly brought her back from what she presumed was an orgasm.

"God damn that was beautiful," he murmured as their gazes clashed together. His eyes full of heat and need.

Without thought, she realized they were swaying back and forth as if in tune to a song only they could hear. By the time he'd stopped moving their bodies side to side, he had her in his bed. The implication was clear.

Or so she thought.

"You'll sleep in here," he paused until she fixed her eyes on him, "with me." He must have seen the stricken look in her stare. "We aren't going to do anything but sleep, Soph. That was phenomenal." His gaze roamed her body. "We'll go slow from now on. I just can't have you in my house and not in my bed. It's not possible."

It was oddly sweet.

"Okay," she managed to say through a tight throat.

His smile was worth all of her nerves, lighting up his entire face. Producing the sexy dimple in his one cheek she had lusted over before.

Relaxing in the bed, she had expected him to go

around to the other side. She was wrong. He scooted in right behind her, wrapping his entire frame around hers. She was cocooned in his muscles, encased in his legs, melting into his embrace.

She felt...

Home.

CHAPTER SEVEN

IT'S NOT WHAT WE HAVE IN LIFE,
BUT WHO WE HAVE IN OUR
LIFE THAT MATTER.

"So, things with Soph, they're real, huh?" Loch asked Nox as they lowered the engine of the Chevelle onto the chassis.

Sophia had spent the past two nights at his place. The first day she'd been nervous about coming into work with him, not wanting to be a burden. When he'd set her to work answering phones and making appointments with Mac, she'd been a nervous wreck. When he told her that morning he was putting her name in the books as an employee, she'd pitched a fit. She hadn't been impressed when he laughed at her either. After he had explained to her that she needed something on her resume, she'd quieted down.

He liked the idea of her being only a few feet away from where he was working so he could see her whenever he wanted.

Before Nox could answer his brother, he overheard the comment, "Sure wish I could bring a piece of tail to work with me. Bang her whenever I like," followed by bouts of laughter as Joey and one of the new painters, Asher, he'd hired walked past him.

Asher wasn't shocked to see him, it's as though he'd expected Joey to hang himself. When Joey saw the storm brewing on Nox's face, he paled. "What's that, Joe?" he asked, not moving from his position bent over the hood of the car. His

white-knuckled grip on the wrench in his hand might have been threatening.

"Uh, nothing, boss," he stuttered.

"Sounded to me like you're either jealous or degrading my woman. Whatcha think, Loch?" He continued tightening a bolt; otherwise, he'd be smacking the fool upside his head.

"You don't wanna know what I think. Chances are the thought would have you doing something reckless and landing your ass in jail." Loch's laughter wasn't appreciated.

"You're probably right." He flicked a look to his brother before standing to his full height. "I think it's a bit of both, and Joey, this'll be your last warning. She's off limits. For anything, to everyone. She's mine, and she damn sure ain't going nowhere. Got it?" Joey nodded and went to walk off when he warned the man, "One more slip up, Joe, and you'll be fired. She's now a full-time employee here. Sexual harassment is a real thing."

The man paled again before scurrying off to do what he'd been assigned that morning already.

"Sorry, boss," Asher said before walking away. He

was a quiet one, lets people hang themselves when necessary. Did what he was told and didn't bitch, so Nox believed him when he said it.

"I'll take that as a yes then." Loch laughed as he wiped his hands clean of grease.

"Take it as a hell yes."

They got back to putting the engine in as the shop quieted down. Some days, he couldn't believe the amount of drama coming from grown ass men, but then he remembered most of the guys were young.

"What do you mean she's not coming home?" Braxton listened as Rebecca kept up her screeching while he and Anthony tried to explain that Sophia likely wasn't coming back.

He couldn't get a solid read on the woman and that, more than anything else, bugged him. She ran hot and cold. She conveyed the right amount of distress as she listened to them, but the emotion was missing from her eyes.

Over the past few days, he'd had a friend digging into her background, financials, and movements. What he'd come up with so far, he didn't like. He had no doubt she was bat shit crazy, he just wasn't prepared for how crazy she could really be. When he'd gotten the rap sheet from when she'd been arrested and charged with stalking at sixteen, he hadn't been shocked. What did surprise him was that the charges were dropped. Not because the accuser had died or mysteriously vanished either, simply dropped.

Rebecca's family wasn't wealthy, so he didn't see them paying it away. It had to be something else. He just couldn't figure out what.

"Why isn't she coming home?" the woman yelled again, this time throwing a crystal vase across the room.

"Rebecca, you need to calm down." Anthony tried to reason with her.

When Brax got a really good look into her eyes, her pupils were dilated, nearly blacking out the whites of her eyes.

"Are you high?" he asked in disbelief. She was a drunk, sure, but he'd never seen evidence of drug abuse.

The rage-filled look she shot his way before launching another vase in his direction gave him the answer he'd suspected as he ducked.

"Anthony, you need to handle this," he warned the man. The woman was clearly off her rocker now.

"What do you care if she's here or not? You don't even like the girl." His boss confronted his wife.

If he thought she was mad before, she was damn near explosive now.

"She is my child. Whether I like her or not is of no consequence."

"Right, so she should take your mental abuse and roll with it?" Brax asked her.

Soph was a sweet girl dealt some shitty fucking parents. He was glad she was taking a stand, though, he suspected it had more to do with Hogan running roughshod over her.

"She ruined my life!" Rebecca screamed.

"How's that now?" Brax asked, knowing that unless he taunted her, he wasn't going to get the answers they would all need. He was only about eighty percent sure she was the one behind the threats.

"She was born!" Rebecca snapped as if the answer was so obvious.

"Your delusional, Rebecca," Anthony snarled at her. Showing the first signs of emotion he had seen since arriving on the scene.

"You couldn't keep it in your pants," she snarled at her husband. "We would have been fine without a child."

"It was your idea!" Anthony yelled back at her.

Color him intrigued.

Dirty secrets were beginning to be revealed.

Sophia had been nervous at first when Lennox had suggested she work in his shop. What did she know about cars? When he said she was going to answer the phones, she'd relaxed a little more, thinking, how hard could it possibly be?

Turned out people only cared that you worked in a shop and not that you had no knowledge of the industry. She'd had one man yell at her for working in a man's world. Another laughed at her incompetence, and a woman told her she'd catch on.

By the time lunch came around, she was exhausted and would be too happy to never answer another phone again. She'd kept that to herself, though, and Lennox was helping her out. She needed something on her resume. She couldn't quit after only two days.

As the clock struck twelve, Lennox walked through the shop door looking sexy as she'd ever seen him. A huge smile on his face as he laughed at something Lochlan said. That dimple she kept noticing made an appearance, and his beautiful blue eyes sparkled with a happiness she envied.

The fact he wore only a muscle shirt and had grease stains all over his body had nothing to do with the squirming she was doing behind the large front desk. Or so she kept telling herself.

"How's it going, good lookin'?" he asked, leaning on the desktop in front of her.

"Oh, you know, kicking ass and taking names." She smiled at her lame joke when he laughed. Straight from the belly and up his chest laughter. Full of life. "It wasn't that funny." Her mouth twisted to the side as she waited for him to calm down.

"Hearing you swear is funny as shit, Soph," he said, tracing her hand with a finger on the desk.

"He's right," Lochlan chimed in.

Looking between the two men, their similarities were so noticeable. If she weren't falling for Nox, she'd think they were twins. Same sandy brown hair, same dark blue eyes, crooked jaws, cleft chins. Their father must have had strong genes because where they were both hard and light, their mother was soft and darker, except for her gray hair, of course.

"Ready for a break?" Nox asked, pulling her around the front of the desk and into his arms.

"Very." She gazed up at him. Seeing the intent in his eyes, her own closed as his lips barely touched hers.

Hearing, "Get a room," broke up the moment and had a growl leaving Nox as he spun to slap his brother.

"Go find Levi and pester his ass," he demanded.

"Can't," Loch told him with a shrug.

"Why the hell not?"

"He's out of town again."

The statement was full of meaning, but she couldn't figure out what or why as they both pondered Lochlan's words.

"Is he okay?" she asked hesitantly.

Neither answered her.

"Let's go grab lunch," Nox suggested again as he guided her out the door with a firm hand on her lower back.

Quickly forgetting her question at his touch, she let him lead her to the small café around the corner. Not once had he lost contact with her until he sat her at a table and went to order for them.

He exuded confidence as he waited in line. Dirty as could be and he was still the best-looking man in the room. Not that she paid attention to anyone else. There was a group of girls around her age sitting on the other side of the café, giggling and pointing towards him. When one girl got to her feet, a look of intent on her face, Sophia stiffened as she approached him.

She stood behind him for a moment before pulling her top down a little further to expose her cleavage. Tapping him on the shoulder, Sophia waited for his devastating smile to grace this other woman. Shock invaded when he dismissed the girl with no more than a curious glance. He didn't smile, didn't engage her in small talk. In fact, he downright scowled at her and turned his back when she tried jiggling her breasts for more attention. Not getting the desired effect, the woman walked back to her table of friends, a look of defeat on her face.

When Lennox turned his attention to Sophia with a smile and a wink, she blushed, deeply satisfied with the entire display. As he placed their order and walked over to where she was sitting, she saw the girls shooting her dirty looks.

"You have some admirers." She nodded in their direction. When his head turned, each of the girls preened and puffed out their chests, as if the only way to get a man's attention was to flaunt their assets.

His scowl returned when he saw what they were doing. "I've got everything I want right here," he told her as he turned back to her.

They spent their lunch in harmonic silence with soft touches and secret looks. Sophia couldn't have been more satisfied with how things were turning out if she had tried.

When she'd run away from home, she hadn't had high hopes of being able to stay away, of succeeding. She'd spent her entire life believing she was stupid. With Lennox, she felt like she could accomplish her goals, as if she were worth more than what she felt. He made her see hope and light at the end of the tunnel, instead of despair. Her only fear was when everything would crash around them like a toppled house of cards.

Watching Soph as she looked around while he ordered gave Nox a chance to see her in a public environment. Observing her discern others let him see how she really felt about certain things. Like he knew when the girl had walked up to him that Soph was expecting the rejection to be aimed at her and not the stranger. When he did brush off the other girl, Soph was shocked.

He hated that she felt like she wasn't good enough. He knew she was having a hard time with talking to so many people at work, and he wouldn't force her to do it if she didn't want to, but he also knew she wouldn't accept a free ride.

Lennox had thought the job was a perfect fit. Mac was up front with her when she would need help answering the technical aspect of things. He had a feeling she wasn't asking for help, though.

While they ate, he stole as many touches of her soft skin as he could. Seeing her small delicate features next to his hardened ones was a huge turn on. He hadn't thought of himself as a caveman before, but with her, it seemed to just come out.

He loved that she was so much smaller than his six-foot frame. That when he wrapped his arms around her, she was engulfed in the width of his shoulders. He felt like he was shielding her from the ugly things in the world. The doubts and fears that were a constant presence in her eyes made him afraid he wouldn't be able to. He knew he was going to have to completely reprogram her to believe the world was intrinsically decent, despite what she'd been led to believe. Not everyone was a complete douchebag like her parents.

"It occurs to me," he began, "that we didn't have that perfect date I had in mind yesterday."

"Maybe we could tonight?" He was glad to see her opening up even just the slightest bit with her question.

"I say, we do it."

Her smile, it was all light and sunshine and life. He'd kill to see the same one on her face for the rest of his life.

Hell, he'd make sure it happened.

They walked back to his shop hand in hand, evening plans set. He couldn't wait for the end of business.

"Hey, boss," Joey called to him from one of the open bay doors. A look of uncertainty on his face. Nox's first instinct was to protect Soph from his sharp tongue. Despite what he'd like to do, he couldn't fire the other man because decent mechanics were hard to find. So, he did his best to keep the man away from her.

"Go on inside, sweetheart, I'll be there in a minute," he told her with a kiss on the cheek. Walking over to the man, he asked, "What's up?"

Joey looked around for a moment before answering. "I'm sorry about being a dick to her. My girl cheated on me, and I've been in a shitty mood." His voice held a hint of fear, confusing Nox.

"Show her respect, and we're good, Joey." He was raised to be the better man.

As he went to turn away, Joey grabbed his arm. "There's someone in there looking for her," he rushed to say.

Not waiting for more information, Nox hurried inside. He didn't know what to expect. Preparing for the worst, he was shocked to see Braxton and her father standing at the front desk. Looking around, he didn't immediately see Sophia.

"Loch took her in your office, boss," Mac told him, apparently catching onto his panic.

"Thanks, Mac." Ignoring the two men standing there waiting, he went straight for his door.

Soph was in his desk chair, bent over. Loch was trying to soothe her.

"What happened?" he barked at his brother.

"She panicked, man. Straight up knees weak, breath gone, deer in the headlights look panicked." Loch sounded every bit as unnerved as she was.

"Thanks, man," he told his brother dismissively.

"Want me to get rid of them?"

He thought about it for a second. The fact that

her father was there gave him pause. "Not yet. Make 'em wait."

As the door closed behind Loch, he knelt in front of his love. Her whispered, "Please don't force me to go back," nearly broke him. Her little body was vibrating with her fear of returning to her cold childhood home.

"Not in a million damn years, baby. You're mine, and there ain't nothing going to change that."

"Why are they here?" Figuring it was a rhetorical question, he remained silent. Pulling her into his arms, they sat on the floor in silence as she got her emotions under control. As much as he wanted to fix everything bad in her life, he knew she had to face this one thing with him by her side. It had to be her choice to stay. If she chose to leave, well then, he'd make the decision for her.

Seeing her father and Braxton in the office as Lennox left to speak to Joey, shook Sophia up more than she ever imagined. Running away from them left her feeling more foolish than anything.

Never in a million years did she expect her father to make an appearance where she was concerned. If anything, she'd half expected her mother to show up with men holding a straitjacket out for her. It wouldn't be shocking if she did at some point, either.

Her father looked...old, sad, when she saw him. Braxton appeared tired and annoyed, which for him she'd quickly learned was normal.

A knock on the door had her head swiveling in that direction as Nox called out, "Come in." Panic sought to threaten her control again as she heard the door open, footsteps enter, and the snick of the latch closing again.

Nox stood to greet who she assumed were her father and Braxton while she remained hidden like a six-year-old. She didn't feel too far off from that age either. She used to hide from her mother all the time. This felt no different.

"Sophia," her father called her name softly.

Closing her eyes, she rose to her feet as Nox grabbed her hand in his, showing his support. She fought to bring her eyes up to meet his. She'd had it beaten into her most of her life that she didn't have or deserve the respect it shows.

When their gazes finally met, the picture she had seen before her made her incredibly sad. Her father had always been a huge imposing presence— larger than life, hard—now, he looked beaten down and despondent. So much so that she rushed to his side. When his arms wrapped around her, held her to his body, she felt the wall of tears she'd been fighting to hold onto for what seemed like years, fall. His fingers dug into her back, and she didn't care because he was holding her, rocking her, treating her like the daughter she never felt she was. There were so many secrets and lies in their home, Sophia hadn't believed she'd ever experience this moment.

"I have some things to tell you, Sophia," he whispered in her ear. His voice full of so much pain and regret it was palpable in the air.

Pulling back, she wiped the tears from her face as Nox walked up behind her, gripping her hips. She could feel the tense muscles in his upper body as her father took a few deep breaths.

"Sit down before you fall down, you fool." Braxton berated the older man.

"I lied when I told you the threat was because of my job," Anthony confessed. She wasn't surprised because, after the text message, she felt like it was personal.

"I figured as much."

Running a weathered hand down his face, she saw regret flash in his eyes before he went on.

165

"There are so many more lies, Sophia. I don't even know where to start."

"From the beginning is always a good idea," Nox suggested, his voice cold. Noticeably unwilling to be as forgiving as her. Not that she could blame the man.

Evidently impatient, Braxton snapped. "Out with it, Anthony. She needs to know."

CHAPTER EIGHT

BE UNDERSTANDING.
BE FORGIVING.
BUT DO NOT BE A FOOL.

Rebecca's not your mother.

Her father's words kept playing over and over in her mind as Lennox drove them to Fort Collins to see the observatory. He wanted to take her home; she wanted to forget the horrors of her life.

It made so much sense. All the hatred the woman felt towards Sophia, the insults. Everything.

Her mother couldn't have children. Her father wanted at least one.

They'd settled on a surrogate.

When her father had begun falling in love with the surrogate, Rebecca became bitter and angry. Irrational.

Anthony and Braxton recently learned that even though there were complications during the birth of Sophia and the surrogate had died, she'd also been poisoned, inducing an early labor. They didn't say it, but she suspected they believed her mother had been behind the poisoning. Probably to make sure her father was stuck with the nasty woman. Making them both endure a life of hatred and anger.

Sophia was torn between feeling pity and anger at the other woman. Imagining the man she married, the man who was supposed to pledge his love and life to you, falling in love with a woman who was giving him the one thing you couldn't, wouldn't have been easy. The pain her mother must have endured watching as her husband slowly drifted away must have gutted her.

Looking over at Lennox, she couldn't begin to imagine what it would be like to lose him that way. Would he want the same thing if she were unable to have children? Would he love her less? He didn't love her now, so she didn't know why she was even thinking about it.

"Whatever that look is about, it needs to stop," he told her, his eyes never leaving the highway.

"What would you do?" she asked quietly.

Nox did look at her then, his eyes understanding. "I'd give you whatever you wanted."

She smiled wanly at him. "Do you think she's behind the threat?" It had crossed her mind on more than one occasion since learning about it.

"I don't think it's something to be ruled out." His answer wasn't committal, and that bothered her. "Soph," his quiet voice drew her attention. "You and me, we're different. We'll be different. Something was wrong with your mom long before you came along."

"I know," she murmured.

She looked up through the windshield as the purr of the engine was cut. Realizing they were at their destination, she looked over to him. "I'm so tired of being sad. Feeling useless. I want something more, Lennox."

She wasn't shocked when he unbuckled her and pulled her onto his lap. His hand entwining her hair in a tight grip, the other hand clenching her thigh under her dress. "You're not useless, Soph." When she attempted to interrupt him, he spoke right over her. "I'm going to make you happy, and if it kills me, I'll give you everything you've never dreamed of, but I already have." A lone tear cascaded down her cheek. "You, Soph, are my dream."

Their mouths clashed in a kiss so intense she felt it to her toes. All her pain, all her fears flew out the window as he made her believe his passionate words. She wanted it all with him. She was ready to experience it all with him.

"I want it all, Lennox," she muttered against his lips.

"You'll get everything you've ever imagined, sugar." His desire matched her own.

"Take me home." Her bold demand had him pulling away.

"You sure?"

"Yes."

It was all the assurance he needed as he re-buckled her, and they left without going into the observatory.

Another time. She smiled.

Excitement drummed through her veins at the thought of giving herself to him. Her eyes were closed as she pictured the way he would strip off her clothes. Kiss his way down her body. His light touches would leave goosebumps in their wake.

Thighs shaking, she tried to quench her thirst for impending pleasure by squeezing her legs together. Hearing Nox groan, "Christ, Soph," had the pleasure drumming through her veins in a faster beat.

After he kissed every inch of her, he would slowly spread her thighs, force her knees to her hips. He'd be hypnotized by her pulsing core just begging for his hot touch.

"Lennox," she moaned out loud.

Feeling his warm hand on her thigh, her eyes slid open to small slits as his fingers lightly trailed up and down her skin.

"More," she whispered, marveled that this vixen was coming forth. She'd never been so bold before.

"You trying to kill me, darlin'?" he groaned, his fingers digging into her thigh possessively.

"I feel so hot," she panted. Her cleansing breaths suddenly gone.

"I'm not taking you on the side of the damn road."

She felt the speed of the car pick up as his fingers grazed across her sex. She pulsed in response. Her body was alight with new sensations she'd never before entertained. He was awakening the woman in her, and she fought between her fear of baring her soul and her desire to connect on an intimate level with him.

The car jerked to a stop, and she heard Lennox's door slam shut before her eyes would open in cooperation just as he opened her door. Pulling her from the vehicle, his lips were on her own in a flash.

It wasn't just a kiss or nibble, he devoured her entire being in the act. His tongue pushed past her startled mouth and tangled with her while his hands had her ass in a bruising grip as he hoisted her up into his hold.

She was so lost in his dominance that she didn't realize they were in the bedroom until he'd dropped them to the bed. His body towered over hers, enveloped her small frame into his muscled chest and arms. She felt so cherished by his forceful move. The way his hands skimmed along her body, swift yet assertive. She knew he was as lost in the sensations as she was.

"Sophia," he groaned into her neck, his hips pushing powerfully against her most intimate area.

Ever so slowly his hand slid her dress up past her waist to settle on her hips. Arching her back as those same strong fingers delved behind her back, she felt the tear as he ripped the zipper open.

Her gasp in the quiet room was audible.

Before she knew it, he had the garment up and over her head. The plop as it landed on the floor the only sound in the room. His eyes, oh, sweet mercy, those deep blue eyes ate her entire body up. She felt electrified as they travelled down her figure. Lingering on her white lace bra, her dusky rose-colored nipples strained for his touch. No words were needed as his hands cupped them, rubbing his thumbs over the peaks, eliciting a moan of pure rapture from somewhere hidden deeply inside of her fighting to break free.

"I don't know where to start." His whispered words were full of reverence and wonder. Her blush was immediate as his hands moved further down her body.

Watching the pleasure work its way across his face and through his body, she felt it as her own. When his hands left her skin, the loss was immediate. Gripping the back of his shirt, he ripped it over his head. All of his glorious muscled form on display. His tan perfection made her mouth water.

His intricate tribal tattoos danced across his chest to his shoulders and wrapped around his back. Chinese symbols marked his ribs, and she wondered what they said until he bent forward to kiss her stomach. She lost all rational thought after that.

"You're like summer and beauty rolled into one sweet package, Soph." The husky note to his voice made her whole body shiver.

Silence shrouded them and every breathy moan from her, every shocked gasp, his guttural groans, they were all magnified. They were the soundtrack to their pleasure.

As he moved slowly but surely down her body, removing the last of her remaining garments, his light kisses and soft touches had her at such a fevered pitch that she could no longer contain herself.

"Please, Lennox," she begged, "I need you."

His smile, so cocky, so sure, held a thousand promises as he stood before her, eyes locked on her own as he stripped the rest of his own clothing off. His thighs were filled with more muscles than she could comprehend. When his boxers dropped to the ground, the thought was forgotten. He was so hard. Large.

"It looks painful."

"It is," her gaze skittered to his when he spoke. She hadn't meant to speak out loud. The rueful grin he had betrayed his amusement.

Crawling back up her body, his hand tickling the insides of her thighs as they searched out her sweet spot. When he finally touched her, when the callouses on his fingers grazed her nether lips she couldn't help the ecstasy-filled cry that left her lips.

She felt him open her up, his heated eyes looking down for one quick second before meeting hers again. "So fucking beautiful."

He made her feel that way. With him, she was everything.

Warmth hit her hard and heavy as his body sunk into hers. He hadn't penetrated her yet, he was savoring the feeling of them together. Their skin touching.

"I've never felt this way before," Sophia whispered into his neck as he nibbled on hers. His lips were soft, his bites added a painful stimulation she found she enjoyed.

"This. Us. It's so fucking right, baby." He didn't move from his position as her legs wrapped around his hips. "This need I have clawing inside of me for you, it's strong. I'm afraid it's going to break you." He did pull back then, his brows etched with worry, his deep bottom of the ocean blue gaze was so intense it stole her breath. "I swear on everything I am though, I'll fucking put you back together."

She felt his cock throbbing against her clit, pounding like a drum. His words played through her mind. Confused her, turned her on.

Placing both of her hands on his sides, she told him, "It's okay, Lennox."

Simple as that. This man, he wanted her. He wanted her for everything she was or wasn't. Bad or good.

He wanted her.

She could handle anything else.

"It's not, though." He sounded almost angry about it. "I want to be buried so deep inside of you, you won't know who we are. I want to own every fucking inch of your soul, Sophia. I want to be so embedded in you that every time you move, every breath you take, you'll think of me. I want you as consumed with thoughts of me as I am of you."

She smiled. She knew what he wanted because she wanted it, too. The uncertainty in his eyes had her speaking up. "When I wake up, it's you on my mind, Lennox. When I fall asleep, it's to the dream of having you wrapped so tightly around me that I can't breathe." The indecision was gone from his gaze, replaced by full obsession. "I want you every bit as much. I just don't know how to show it."

Her body squirmed as he began sliding up and down her slit. The heat coming from his body almost her undoing as each stroke hit her nub.

"I'm gonna enter you now, sweetheart. It's gonna be the sweetest pain you'll ever feel." She could only nod her head as he slid one finger in, stretching her walls. A slight burn ensued when a second joined the first.

"You're burning up," he groaned.

"Nox." Her breath hissed out as he touched something deep inside of her.

"Oh, yeah, baby, we're gonna light it up." She didn't know what he meant until she felt the head of his cock begin to push inside of her.

He was thick, hard.

Sweet mercy. The pressure as he slowly intertwined their bodies.

The burn turned to agony as he thrust completely inside of her. "I'm fucking sorry, Soph." His words were just as pained as her body.

"I know," she croaked.

His hands had somehow managed to delve into her hair, pulling with each labored breath from his body. His lips rained kisses on her neck, soothing her overwhelmed mind. When he adjusted his body so his knees were on either side of her hips, forcing her legs higher on his, he tapped that spot inside her again, and bliss zinged through her entire being. A gasp of surprise left her when he slowly began moving.

His obsession was growing. This driving force within Lennox that screamed he had to dominate and own every fucking inch of her body and soul was overwhelming. When he'd told her what he wanted, he didn't think for a second she would reciprocate. He thought for sure she'd run off. Push him away.

She didn't.

She confessed to feeling the exact same way.

Seeing her naked body had done something to his mind, the caveman in him had burst forth, demanded they have her. Love her. Now, as he moved slowly inside of her, giving her all the pleasure he could while she gasped for breath, he was glad he'd let that piece of him out.

Nox's body surrounded Sophia so completely there was no space between them. His arms bracketed her shoulders and head, his knees were pressed tightly to her hips. Their bodies were connected from shoulder to thigh, sweat coated them as his thrusting picked up speed. Their gazes stayed connected, heat and fire blasting between them. Her pupils were dilated with desire. She was his. Her feet dug into the backs of his thighs, urging him to go faster and deeper while her fingers stroking up and down his sides had a shiver of ecstasy racing through him.

The slow slide in and out of her tight little pussy allowed him to feel every wave of rapture as it tore through her. When she tightened, he would move the same way again. Her squirming had him pumping in just a little bit harder. As her breaths stalled in her chest and her body tensed, he knew she was about to come apart.

Leaning the rest of the way down, his lips took control of hers as his hands moved down to grip the tops of her thighs, keeping her in place as he took her over the edge into a frenzy of carnality. He devoured her screams of pleasure as her hands tightened on his shoulders while he felt her walls explode with the force of the orgasm ripping through her small figure. One more deep stroke inside of her as she continued falling apart before him, and he was exploding his life's force into her willing body.

"Fuck, Soph," he groaned into her mouth, nipping her bottom lip as he lost power over his own massive release. A surge of pleasure detonated through him like a rocket when her body arched beneath him, tightening around his cock as the last of his cum emptied inside of her.

As the rush of bliss left his body, his muscles turned to jelly. Collapsing on top of her, he felt a new spark of hope while her limbs moved along him. A purr of contentment worked through her as he turned them on their sides to face each other. The look on her face, pure delight, was enough for him to know she'd enjoyed their lovemaking.

"That was incredible," she murmured, her eyes heavy with sleep.

Pushing the hair back from her face and tangling his fingers in the gold locks, he told her, "I like you like this." He kissed her forehead. "Sated." He dropped another on her cheek. "Happy." Another on the tip of her nose. "Mine." Before finally taking her lips with more passion than he thought himself capable of after such an intense coupling.

Falling asleep with her in his arms, the scent of their loving surrounding them, Nox had never felt so complete in his life.

He found her.

The one woman to make him love stupid.

She'd be his everything.

Looking down at her sleeping face full of love and life, Nox couldn't be happier than he was in that moment as she let out a contented sigh.

Sophia was life.

CHAPTER NINE

STOP TRYING SO HARD FOR PEOPLE
WHO DON'T CARE.

SOPHIA AWOKE the next morning deliciously sore in all the right areas. For once, she didn't feel an ounce of uncertainty about what they'd done the night before. Giving Nox her body was one of the best choices she'd ever made.

The way he'd held her as they made love, the protection from the world as he devoured her body made her heart crack wide open. She was falling in love with him and heaven help her, she wanted to. She wanted him to be the one person in the world that belonged to her.

Fairytale love had never been an inkling of an idea for her before. She'd never believed in the all-consuming, mind changing emotion. Seeing Lorraine's love for her husband and then her sons had her mind opening up to the idea.

Meeting Lennox and his over-bearing personality, she was definitely a believer now. She still had her hectic life to work through. She had to find out why someone wanted to hurt her before she could even think about letting her emotions develop into full-blown love. She couldn't give him a false promise if she didn't know what the future held.

Hearing his groan next to her, a huge smile worked across her face. He was still there. For some reason, she thought she'd wake up alone. Feeling his fingers work across her belly to grab her hip, he pulled her into his body. He was warm, relaxed as he kissed her shoulder.

"Good morning, beautiful." His husky words followed by his swollen member digging into her butt made her giggle.

Before she could say a word, his alarm clock and phone started going off simultaneously causing him to groan with frustration while nipping her shoulder where his lips had been. "Hey!" she admonished him as he stood from the bed.

Her eyes nearly bulged from her head seeing his naked body in the sunlight streaming through the curtain. His butt had to be sculpted from marble with its perfection. The ease with which he walked around, uncaring that she could see every imperfection in his body, not that she'd found any, made her green with envy.

One day she would have the confidence, she hoped.

The shower starting was her cue to leave the bed in search of her clothes. Seeing her tattered dress on the floor, she grabbed Nox's shirt beside it. As she slipped the garment over her head, she walked into the bathroom.

"Care to join me?" he asked from the open shower door.

Blushing profusely, she admitted, "I'd like to keep the aches a little longer. Makes it real."

The heated look and enormous grin on his face showed his immense satisfaction at her answer. She listened to his smug whistling while she brushed her teeth and hair. As he climbed from the shower, her eyes were glued to his reflection in the mirror. Watching him dry off, the water dripped down his muscular chest. Sophia had the urge to lick every drop free before it could be absorbed from his skin. She was lost in a trance as the rivulets worked their way down his body to his muscular thighs and all the way to his strong feet.

Feet that were moving.

Towards her.

"Oh," she gasped as his front hit her back. His hands held hers on the counter. When their eyes finally clashed in the mirror, she was putty in his hands.

"Like what you see, Soph?" he groaned into her neck.

Coherent thought wasn't something she could process. He was taking over her mind, hitting every pleasure sensor in her body without even trying.

"I like how you watch me, baby." His hips pushed into her from behind as he nibbled on her ear lobe.

Her eyes closed of their own volition when his hands roamed up her arms and across her chest. Pulling her much smaller frame back into him, he gripped her shirt in both fists, whipping it over her head before she was aware of it happening.

"Open your eyes," he hissed into her ear.

She struggled to do as he commanded, knowing it would be her nude body in the mirror rather than his. "Open 'em, Soph." His hands tightened around the ribs where he held her.

When she finally gave in, the heat of his gaze as he met hers stole her breath. An intense fervor of passion blazed back at her. He didn't care that she wasn't a tight, compact package. His hands grazed her ribs as she shivered in his embrace. He loved every plush curve of her body.

When she was about to say something, the doorbell rang, startling them from their intimate moment. His hands gripped her belly, forcing her further back into him as he placed a kiss on her shoulder. "I'll go get that." The air left the room with him.

She could breathe again, only she didn't think she wanted to. When Lennox held her, it was the only time anything made sense to her. She` made sense. The feelings he brought forth in her were so real and turbulent she didn't think she'd be able to function without them any longer.

Lennox was an addiction she didn't know existed.

Sophia left Nox breathless more often than not for so many different reasons. The uninhibited passion she had locked away inside of her was his favorite, though. The way she'd come apart for him when they'd made love still left his mind blown. She had a fire deep inside. An inferno so consuming that he knew he would fight to keep it stoked for the rest of his life.

Leaving her naked in the bathroom so he could answer the door left him frustrated on so many levels. The primary annoyance right now was the erection he was trying to convince to disappear as he slowly made his way to the door.

Just as he opened it, a fist nearly came crashing down on his face. "Jesus Christ," he cursed, seeing Levi, once again, beaten to shit. "What the fuck is going on, Levi?" He had caught his little brother's pain-filled form before he collapsed in the doorway.

"I can't, Nox." The grief in the other man's voice was soul deep. Whatever was going on with his life, Nox recognized that the younger man still had some working out to do.

"You can't keep showing up like this, bro. Has Ma seen you?"

"Haven't been there since the weekend." His voice was scratchy like he'd been smoking a pack a day for twenty years.

"Oh my gosh!" Sophia's shocked voice had them both spinning to face her. "What happened? Are you okay?" He watched, fascinated as her motherly instincts kicked in while she fussed over Levi.

"I'm fine, Soph," he wheezed out, nearly doubling over in pain.

"Sit your ass down before you fall down," Nox told him.

"I'll go make coffee and get ice." Sophia skittered off.

"Why are you so bitchy?" Levi asked him as he sat on the couch.

Nox levelled him with a look that only another man would ever understand.

"Sorry, man."

Sitting beside him, Nox struggled with how to handle this situation. He needed to know what was going on with his brother, but he didn't want to push so hard that Levi started pushing back.

"Tell me you have things under control, at least?"

He shrugged. A fucking shrug.

If the man didn't look so damn beat up, Nox would have kicked his ass.

"You got someone to talk to? Something, Levi."

"Yeah, I got someone," he answered quietly as Soph came into the room with a bag of ice. Worry etched every line of her face.

She had enough shit to worry about, she didn't need to worry about his dip-shitted brother, too. As soon as she walked out of the room after handing him the ice pack, he told Levi, "She's got enough on her plate."

"I know."

"Don't fucking make her worry about you, too," Nox warned, punching his shoulder hard enough to have him cowering away.

"Fuck, man, I got it."

"Let this shit heal then go see Ma," he instructed his brother.

"Why you pushing that?" he asked Nox with the ice against his eye.

"Because even if she doesn't know what's going on, maybe she can still talk your dumb ass into some common sense before something worse happens to you."

Leaving the room, he went in search of his girl. Finding her in the kitchen with a cup of coffee in hand and eggs on the burner, he knew she was concerned when she didn't so much as look up at his entrance.

"Hey, baby," he cooed in her ear. Having her body dwarfed by his was such a turn-on. He couldn't get enough of the sight they presented together. Watching her in the mirror after his shower, seeing the astonished look on her face when he made her open her eyes had him hard enough to pound nails.

And he would have, if not for fucking Levi.

"Is he alright?" she asked him, cuddling into his hold.

"Not a clue." Breathing her scent in was far more appealing than talking about his battered sibling.

A loud pop had Sophia racing from his hold to check the food she had on the burner. Turning, he took a sip of her coffee, grimacing at the sweet taste. "Way too much sugar," he commented as she plated the eggs she made and some toast. "You're allergic to eggs," he pointed out needlessly as she walked to the living room. "Where's mine?" he called after her.

"That was yours," she laughed.

"Bastard brother," he cursed again.

"They're burnt," she told him when she saw he was sulking. "You'll get more."

Having her in his home, cooking his food, was a sight he could get used to. If he had his way, they'd remain like this forever.

His phone ringing broke him from admiring her yet again. He was beginning to think living in the pre-technology era wouldn't be so bad.

"What?" he snapped into the receiver.

"Yo, boss, that bitch is back," Mac greeted.

"What bitch?" He was confused.

"Your girl's mom. She's going at Asher. This shit ain't gonna end well." Mac sounded like he was fighting off laughter.

While Asher was a pretty quiet guy, his intensity told another story. All was not well in his world, and as much as he'd like to let the man go at the bitch Bennett, his conscience wouldn't allow for it. "I'll be there as soon as I can." Hanging up before Mac could respond, he looked at a curious Sophia. "I've gotta get to work, baby."

"Give me five, and I'll be ready." She gave him a bright smile.

He hated what his words were going to do to that radiance. "I need you to stay here today, Soph. Something is going on I have to deal with."

"Oh." Her smile faded. "What is it?"

"There's someone there right now. She's causing a fuss. I don't want you around that." He was omitting the truth, and he felt horrible.

"My mother?" Her perceptive question made him kind of sad for her. Imagining what she'd had to deal with growing up to even think that was who the problem was.

"Yeah."

"I'll come."

She was gone before he could say a word of protest.

Planting his hands on his hips, his tilted back, he blew out a breath, mumbling, "This *really* isn't going to end well," before following her upstairs to finish dressing.

The drive to Lennox's shop was short and quiet after they got Levi settled in the spare room to rest. Time

Sophia needed to gather her resolve and fortify any cracks in her composure. She knew as soon as her mother saw her, the insults and accusations would fly. All the guys she'd worked so hard to get to like her would hear the lies, and she would become tainted again. As much as the idea made her sick to her stomach, she knew she had to take a stand against Rebecca. Having Nox by her side gave her the strength she was going to need to come to terms with the eventual loss of her parent.

Pulling up, all looked calm, but she knew her mother. Sophia recognized the woman as a viper in swans' clothing. Elegant and beautiful on the outside, venomous and malicious on the inside.

Slowly exiting the car, she followed behind Lennox as he pulled the front door open. And that's when they heard it.

"You're so cute, I bet you know how to show a girl a good time." If she were hitting on the guys, that meant they hadn't given her what she wanted. Which meant next stage was pure rage.

"Rebecca!" Nox snapped. His repulsion for the woman couldn't be masked.

"Lennox," she hissed. Clearly angry with the man.

"You need to leave," he told her while Sophia hid off to the side.

"My daughter needs to come home," she bit back.

"Why?" Sophia spoke before thinking it through. When her mother's cold gaze swung to her, she fought every instinct she could to not shrink away.

"Because," the older woman walked closer to her, forcing Soph to back up in an effort to create distance between them, "you belong at home." Lennox had grabbed Rebecca's arm before she reached Sophia.

"You don't even like me, why would I come home?"

"You belong to me." Her words were low and venomous, reminding her of the viper she'd always compared the woman to.

"I don't..." she struggled to defend herself. "I don't belong to anyone."

Looking into her mother's eyes, the crazy light in them had her worried. The sounds she began making as she fought to get out of Lennox's hold made her cringe. They were inhuman. Malevolent almost.

"I raised you; I brought you into this world. I can damn well take you out, you stupid girl!" She was sure the woman's screams and accusations could be heard across the state.

"Why?" She shouted back, tired of being the whipping girl in her mother's tirades. "You hate me so much, why keep me? Why not have given me away or killed me all those times we were alone?" Saying the words annihilated a part of her soul. "You keep calling me stupid. All my life it's been, Stupid Sophia! Stupid, stupid, stupid!" Breath left Sophia's body in erratic spurts as she fought back for the first time in her life. "Well, fuck you! You're the stupid one! You can't see a good thing right in front of your face. You can't get past your own vanity to see anything but greed." Walking closer, Sophia leaned into the woman, so they were nearly nose to nose. "Get out and don't ever come back." Her words were whispered but no less impactful than when she was shouting.

Ears ringing as her temper faded, she barely noticed Asher and Mac escorting the woman out the front doors. Lennox's arms wrapped around her, and the tension left her body in a rush.

"I think I need to sit down," she muttered into his chest.

Picking her up, he took her to his office and sat her on the couch. When she started hyperventilating, he forced her head between her legs. Rubbing soothing circles on her back, he encouraged with, "Slow breaths, Soph."

"Joey!" She cringed at his call.

"Yeah, boss?" Was it her, or was everyone yelling?

"Stop yelling," she cried as tears rolled down her face.

Am I having a panic attack? she idly wondered.

"No one's yelling, baby." Nox mumbled in her ear, laying a light kiss on her cheek.

"Crap," she muttered.

She still had a hard time believing she stood up to her mother. The woman had been a menacing force her entire life. She'd never been able to fight back against the insults. She'd taken it, rolled over and played dead her whole life.

Standing up for herself was...freeing.

Exhilarating.

Cathartic.

Terrifying.

What if that woman was behind the threats against her? What if she upped her game and came after Sophia with more than threats?

"Sweetheart, take a drink." Nox held a water bottle out for her. After a quick sip, the cool liquid helped calm some of her nerves. Not everything, though, because now all she could think about was her mother attacking her.

"She's behind everything, isn't she?" The quiet in the room confirmed her suspicions.

A knock on the door followed by, "Boss, they're here," had her finally sitting up straight.

"Mr. Hogan." Her father walked in with Braxton right behind him.

"You still want to protect Soph, I assume." Nox pulled no punches with that comment.

"Of course." Her father's brows furrowed in consternation.

"Your wife is off her fucking rocker. Get her committed and find out what the fuck she has planned for your daughter. After today, I can guarantee things will go to shit. Whatever the fuck you did, you need to fix." His words left no room for argument.

"What happened?" Braxton asked before her father could.

"What happened is that cunt came into my shop, caused a shit storm of trouble with my employees then sweet little Soph found her backbone and basically invited the bitch to kill her." His angered words made her think back to her own, and she couldn't deny it.

"Oh, what did I do?" she moaned into her hands as she covered her face.

"Relax, Soph." Nox still sounded so angry with her.

"You need me to stick around?" Braxton asked, his question directed at her.

How did she say yes without it sounding like she didn't trust Lennox to keep her safe?

"Yes," Nox blurted before she could answer. Relief swamped her as he exerted control once again. When he took over, she didn't feel like the burden she'd always felt like at home. With him, she considered herself an equal half of a whole.

"Done." Her father agreed. "Sophia?" He waited until she looked at him before saying to her, "I'm sorry you're caught up in this. I'm sorry I haven't protected you better."

"Me too," she whispered back as he stood to leave.

"When this is all over, I would like to try again to be the father you deserve. If you'll let me?" The sheer emotion emitting from his words spoke to his sincerity, and she knew she would give anything to make sure they had the chance for a do-over.

"I'd like that." She gave him a faint smile.

"I'll be back tonight. I'm going to scope out your

neighborhood and check the tracking device I have on Rebecca's car. See where she's been the past few days," Braxton informed them before leaving with her father.

As the door closed behind them, her breath left her in a whoosh. When Nox said, "I'm so fucking pissed at you, Soph," tears pooled in her eyes.

"I'm sorry," she replied, not even having to ask what he was angry about.

"Why would you do that? Knowing how fucked up she is."

"I don't know."

His body crowded hers as he pushed her back on the sofa. "And you're dead fucking wrong about one thing, sugar," he growled into her throat, stealing her breath as he began kissing her.

"What?" She asked breathlessly.

"You do belong to someone." His kisses were more demanding as he began sucking her skin.

"I do?"

"Me, Soph. Every delectable inch of this gorgeous body is mine. All" *kiss* "Fucking" *suck* "Mine."

"Okay." She acquiesced to his command.

CHAPTER
TEN

IF YOU WANT TO KNOW WHERE YOUR
HEART IS, LOOK WHERE YOUR MIND
GOES WHEN IT WANDERS.

Every thought, every decision Nox made was with Sophia in mind. When she wasn't near, it was all he could do not to hunt her down. She was at her weekly book chat with his mother discussing some new romance he had no idea how she found the time to read.

After their first night together, the first time he took her, he'd been insatiable. When they weren't working or fueling up on energy, he'd had her pinned to the bed. Or wall. The counter twice while she was cooking for him. Damn was that a fucking turn-on he'd never expected.

The woman was a seductive siren with her innocence. The cute dresses she always wore. She was girly to the core, and he couldn't be happier with it. Seeing his grease-stained hands on her perfect porcelain skin never failed to light his fire.

"Nox, you paying attention?" Loch bitched at him.

They were supposed to be watching an NHRA race, but he kept zoning out.

"Yeah," he grumbled taking another sip of his beer.

For the first time in his life, the quarter-mile just didn't interest him. The thought of fucking Soph on the hood of his car at the track, however, fueled yet another fantasy.

"Dude, you're pussy-whipped." Loch laughed.

With any other man, he'd clean their clock for even thinking of his woman like that; fortunately, he knew Loch was busting his balls.

Besides, it was completely true. She had him wrapped around her tiny little finger, and he wouldn't change a damn thing about it.

Checking his watch again, he still had another hour before he had to pick her up. He was almost annoyed with his mom for demanding her time. She was his. Plain and simple. He didn't want to share her with anyone.

His mother was a force to be reckoned with, and he knew that if he ever wanted to live in peace with his girl, he'd have to concede to some things with the older woman.

Like sharing.

"You could just knock her up, and Ma wouldn't try stealing her from you anymore. She'd take the baby," Loch suggested, laughing.

It wasn't a bad idea.

"You're thinking about it." His brother laughed harder. "You can't be that obsessed with the girl."

"You'll find out, Loch. You find that girl that

steals your breath with just a look, and you won't be laughing no more."

A faraway look entered his brother's eyes, making Nox wonder if he'd already found her.

"You've found her, haven't you?"

Loch shrugged.

"Tell me about her." Nox pushed.

"Can't." Loch took a long chug of his beer.

"Why the hell not?" he demanded.

"She's underage. Don't matter who she is. Can't touch her."

Nox was speechless as he watched his youngest brother's heartache. Loch was a different breed of man compared to him and Levi. He was more sensitive, empathetic. He understood far more than either he or Levi ever could.

Knowing Loch had a girl out there, and one that he couldn't act on made him ache for the younger man. The hurt he must feel not having her at his side. Well, call him selfish, but it made Nox want to have Soph in his arms that much more.

Following his brother to the kitchen, he clapped a hand on his shoulder, asking him, "Have you spoken to her?"

"Not once."

"Damn."

"Pretty much, yeah. Can't do anything for I don't know how long, and I can see it's killing her inside as well. I can see the ache in her eyes, the sadness when I have to leave the room or risk going to jail for claiming her before she's legal." His words held all the pain he felt.

"So, she knows about you?"

"Yup." The hiss of the can of beer being opened the only sound in the room.

"What are you gonna do?"

"Not a fucking clue. Worst part is, I think her parents already have her married off when she is legal. Maybe even before then."

"Before then? How is that even possible?"

"She's from that religious compound an hour out from here."

That put a wrinkle in things.

"Can't she leave? Don't they have something where the kids can move out on their own for a while when they're eighteen, choose where they want to live or something?"

"Beats me." He could tell Loch was done with the conversation as he walked out of the room.

Seemed to Nox now, he likely wasn't the only one with girl trouble. He had his girl under control.

Watching his younger brothers fall was gonna be fun.

His phone ringing had all traces of amusement leaving his system at the terrifying words were blasted at him.

There's been an accident.

"So tell me, Sophia, how are things going with my boy?" Lorraine's question threw her off guard. She knew the woman would eventually ask her about how quickly things had been moving, but she hadn't known when.

"Umm, well, good, I think. I hope," Sophia responded honestly.

"You think?" She had to remember Lorraine didn't know what had transpired between her and her mother. The accusations, the truths and lies, all the scary things that could happen. Lorraine was in the dark.

"Between us is good. At work is good." She looked away before saying, "It's my family that's not so good."

"Well, we always knew they'd be a problem. Especially that jealous mother of yours." Lorraine's lip curled in disgust as she mentioned the other woman.

"It's uh, well, become a little more complicated in the last couple of weeks." She stuttered over her words.

"What do you mean?" her friend asked, understandably confused.

"Lennox told you there was a threat?" Lorraine nodded. "Turns out it was aimed directly at me, not my father, and I think it comes from my mother." Saying it out loud still hurt like hell.

"Why would you think that?" In the Hogan's world, Sophia could understand how unfathomable it seemed. Because who really wants to harm their child? How she wished that could be her world, too.

"I guess I'm not really hers. Dad wanted kids, Mom wanted money. They got a surrogate, but my mother was sterile, so, from what I've been told, they used the surrogate's eggs. Turns out this vile woman isn't really my mother. She spent her entire life making my father regret bringing me into this world with how vicious she's been. She made my life miserable solely because she could." Tears stung her eyes.

"But why would she do this now?" Lorraine moved to sit beside her, gripping her hands tightly in her own for comfort. Sophia relished the affection.

"I have no clue. Maybe she finally sees a way to truly hurt one of us. Or maybe she's simply mentally unhinged. Maybe she's plotted this for years. I doubt I'll ever know."

"Is that why that delicious hunk of meat is sitting outside my door?"

It took Sophia a moment to realize the older woman was talking about Braxton. Laughter bubbled up thinking of him as a hunk. "Yes, that's why he's here." She couldn't stop laughing; eventually, Lorraine joined in with her.

Once they ran out of breath, things turned serious again. "So, what's being done? Are the police investigating? Is your father finally going to divorce the wretched woman?"

Thinking back on all the conversations they'd had, she didn't remember mention of police involvement. Most of the time, she had been stunned by the new information thrown at her, so she couldn't be sure.

"I assume the police are involved. I know Brax has men following my mother and digging through her entire life with a fine-tooth comb. They did discover she was obsessed with someone back before Dad. Charges were withdrawn, though."

"Maybe it's time your father and I had a talk about this whole situation." It seemed as though she was thinking out loud and not actually speaking to Sophia.

"Oh no, please don't. My mother will come completely unglued. I'd hate for something to happen to you because of me, Lorraine." She would rather die a thousand deaths before letting harm come to the sweet woman who had treated her with nothing but kindness and compassion.

Patting her hand, Lorraine assured her, "It will all be fine, dear, you'll see."

Letting it go because she knew how stubborn Nox and his brothers could be, she mentioned the book they were supposed to have read the past two weeks. As they spoke about the good and the bad, ups and downs, Sophia couldn't help thinking of all the trouble she was causing with so many people.

She wasn't a martyr, not by a long shot, but she wondered if maybe she should confront her mother on her own. Get everything out in the open. Find out what the hell was really going on because she had a sense there was more than just hatred between them. Something deeper.

Before she knew it, their time was coming to a close and Braxton was knocking on the door. "Braxton, huh? Different name," Lorraine commented, a teasing gleam in her eye.

"Nice to meet you, ma'am." He looked uncomfortable.

"Next time come inside. No sense sitting out here alone."

"I like the quiet." He was nearly squirming.

"I'll see you soon, Lorraine," Sophia interrupted.

Leaning in to give her a hug, she whispered in her ear, "Stay safe, dear."

Nodding, Sophia followed Braxton down the front steps and to the waiting town car. She'd insisted Lennox spend the afternoon with his brothers, knowing he was worried about Levi and whatever was going on with him.

"Hungry?" Braxton asked her as he opened the door.

"Not really," she told him. There was too much weighing on her mind as they left the quiet neighborhood.

The drive to Lennox's house was a short one. They were only two blocks away when an impact so jarring had every window in the car shattering. Her head bounced off the door frame, her ears were ringing and her head swimming as she tried to stop the spinning in her vision.

"Sophia!" She heard Braxton yelling her name but couldn't answer. She could barely move. Pain vibrated through her entire body as her world turned black.

Arriving on the scene of the crash, Nox had never been so glad he and his brothers lived so close together. The screeching of his brakes was nearly deafening as he and Loch barreled from the barely parked vehicle.

The carnage, the glass, the natural smell of gas had his stomach rolling over. Searching the littered road for Sophia, he was freaking out when he couldn't see her. He prayed it wasn't as bad as it looked.

"Nox!" His head whipped around at the call of his name. Seeing Braxton near an ambulance, he rushed over to the other man. Blood ran down the side of his face, and his arm was in a sling.

"What the fuck happened?" he screamed, his temper getting the best of him. "Where the fuck is Soph?"

Remorse shot from the man's eyes as he looked to the ambulance across from where they were standing. Rushing over, Loch hot on his heels, he looked inside the vehicle. What he saw had his knees so weak with fear, Loch had to grip his arm to keep him upright.

Laying on a stretcher was his Sophia.

Blood covering the entire upper half of her body.

Her chest red from the catch of her seatbelt.

Her arm in a sling, and her leg being stabilized by a board.

The worst part was all the glass protruding from her cheek, neck, and shoulder. The golf ball sized bump on the side of her head.

"Sir?" One of the paramedics called to him.

"Yeah?"

"You the boyfriend we were warned about."

He looked sideways at Brax who shrugged before he answered, "Yeah."

"Good. Let's go," he demanded.

"I got your car," Loch told him.

Climbing into the back of the ambulance, he sat on the bench next to his broken love. Getting a closer look at her injuries, anger infused his blood.

"They know who did this?" he asked the medic.

"Car hit 'em on her side and took off. Police are looking now," he explained quietly.

He had to force the question out. "She gonna be okay?"

"As long as there's no internal bleeding and no bruising on her brain, yeah, I think so." Compassion colored the man's words.

"What are her injuries right now? Is her leg broken?" Christ, he wasn't gonna be able to handle seeing her in pain.

"For sure, concussion, broken wrist, whiplash, severe bruising to her shoulder and abdomen from the seat belt. Which is where internal injuries can occur. As for her leg, not broken, but a piece of plastic from the inside door dug into her calf pretty deeply, and I wanted her immobile, so it doesn't keep bleeding."

"Fuck." He scrubbed his face with his hands. "What about the other guy? He gonna be okay?" As much as Brax got on his nerves, the man was protecting his girl so he couldn't hate him too bad.

"Concussion, sprained arm, and whiplash. Miss Bennett took the brunt of the impact." He didn't feel better.

Gripping her limp hand in his own, he kissed

her soft knuckles. Hating that she was so injured. Hating that he wasn't there to protect her.

"Here we are," the medic told him as the vehicle slowed and the back doors were opened. A team of doctors was waiting for her as the paramedic listed off her injuries in medical jargon he was having a hard time processing.

He followed along until a nurse held him back, telling him, "You'll have to wait here, sir."

"No, I need to be with her," he insisted.

"The doctors need to look her over. We have a dozen tests to run, and you'll only be in the way." She pulled him away from the doors that his girl had disappeared behind, handing him a clipboard. "Fill these out. By the time you're done, someone will come out with news on her condition." She walked away before he could protest again.

Standing in the middle of the E.R., he was lost. For the first time in his life, he had something to lose that meant more to him than anything else in the world. Sophia was his entire existence. If he lost her, if she didn't come back to him, he didn't know what the hell he'd do.

"Nox?" A hand on his shoulder startled him. Seeing his brothers there with him, relief swamped in.

"How is she?" Levi asked, looking around as if she were there.

"I don't know yet. She was taken back, and I was given these." He clapped the board against his palm.

"I'll fill that out," Loch grabbed it from him. "Call her dad."

"Braxton's done that, I'm sure. Besides, with all this shit, I don't think I can see him and not kick his ass. You call Ma?" he asked them.

"Yeah, said she was going to clean up your old room for Soph, so she had someone to take care of her when she gets out." As much as he'd like to dispute her idea, he knew she needed something to do besides worry. Aside from that, he knew he was going to need help taking care of her after she left the hospital.

If she left the hospital.

"Don't think like that, man." Levi levelled him with a hard glare.

"Like what?" he retorted, on edge.

"Like she ain't coming home. She's tougher than you think, Nox."

Yeah, she was. She was made of tougher stuff than anyone gave her credit for. She felt just as strongly.

"I can't fucking lose her," he mumbled as his

brother led him to a row of empty chairs in the otherwise busy room.

"You won't," he insisted.

Lennox watched the clock as they waited, and every minute felt like an hour. An hour longer than he should be kept away from her. An hour longer that he had no information. Agonizing about whether something went wrong or not while he was left in the dark.

As he was about to demand answers, a nurse came from behind the doors Soph had been taken through. "Mr. Hogan?" she asked.

"Yeah, that's me."

"Come with me, please. You can see Miss Bennett now."

Tossing his phone to Levi, he said, "Call Braxton, find out where the hell they are."

Trepidation had his steps slowing as the nurse opened a door. Taking a fortifying breath, he entered the room. Beeping sounds and a hushed voice were the only audible noise. Walking closer to the bed in the middle of the room, he was shocked at how pale she looked, how many machines surrounded her.

"You're the boyfriend?" he was asked for a second time that day.

"Yeah," his voice cracked as he saw the bruising on her face.

"It looks much worse than it is, so take a deep breath and sit down." The doctor laughed. Nox found nothing funny.

"What do the tests say?" he asked her, looking up. She was an older woman. Thin, graying hair, kind eyes. Reminded him a bit of his mom.

"Miss Bennett suffered some severe bruising along her chest and belly. Thankfully, there is no internal bleeding which is always the biggest worry. She'll heal from that just fine, but it will take a while. Her wrist is broken, and she'll be getting that set just as soon as she wakes up on her own, and then we can put her under again. We need to know her cognitive function before we can do that because of the concussion."

His head was swimming with the information.

Clearing his throat, he asked, "The concussion, how bad is it?"

She hesitated for a second before answering. "The good news is there's no bleeding so far."

"And the bad news?"

"There's some swelling."

"What does that mean?"

217

"If there's too much cranial pressure, we may have to drill a hole in her skull to relieve it."

"Christ, baby." Tears. For the first time in his life, he was close to shedding a tear.

His girl was so fucking broken.

"Don't worry just yet, Mr. Hogan. We're not there at this time. We'll continue to monitor her progress." She placed a hand on his shoulder in a display of support before leaving him alone to contemplate what the fuck he was going to do.

"Come back to me, sweetheart." He kissed the tip of each finger on her uninjured hand as a tear rolled silently down his cheek.

"You stupid bitch! You've ruined everything." Rebecca snarled at the woman who was to blame for everything. She had been perfectly fine hating Sophia, tormenting her and her father for forcing the girl into her life. Now, this spoiled brat from Sophia's biological mother showed up. She was ruining Rebecca's plans to get her hands on all of Anthony's money.

"Maybe you shouldn't have killed our mother." The bitch had the audacity to snarl back at her.

"Listen here, little girl, we didn't even know you existed."

"Because that gives you the right to kill another human being." Her sarcasm wasn't missed.

Rebecca eyed her up. She was a tiny thing, completely opposite of Sophia in looks with her amber hair, but the eyes...they were exact same shade as Sophia's.

"What do you want?" she barked at the little blackmailer.

"My sister." She crossed her arms with impatience.

"How much will it take to make you go away?" Rebecca had tried bargaining with the young woman months ago, but she just wouldn't leave well enough alone. That's when she had come up with the idea of making threats against Sophia, getting Anthony worried enough he had hired protection for the brat.

She had intended on framing the shit standing before her; unfortunately, nothing worked out as planned. Although, after the accident, she still might be able to. She only had to get Elianna's fingerprints in her own car. Find a way to make it look like she was trying to set them all up. Hurt Anthony for not sticking around, and Sophia for taking the life she never had.

"I told you from the beginning, I don't want anything from your vile ass."

Rebecca sneered at the woman, already planning her demise. It wouldn't be the first time she'd blackmailed someone. Or taken a life. She only had to plant the seed of doubt in Anthony's mind so he would start looking anywhere but at Rebecca.

CHAPTER
ELEVEN

WE FALL IN LOVE BY CHANCE.
WE STAY IN LOVE BY CHOICE.

THE SMELL OF ANTISEPTIC, a loud beeping, and pain radiating through her entire body had Sophia trying to open her eyes. Fighting with her mind over where she was and what had happened.

As soon as a bright light hit her pupils, she moaned, slamming her lids shut again. The pain was unlike anything she'd felt before. Taking a few deep breaths, she tried moving her hands to shield her eyes from the brightness, but a sharp tug on her wrist had her hissing through her teeth.

"Soph?"

Nox, she sighed.

"Don't move, darlin'. I'll get the nurse." When she felt his hand on hers, she squeezed as tight as she could so he wouldn't leave her. "Baby, I gotta get the nurse." He sounded pained.

"Please stay," she whispered, at least she thought she did. Her mouth moved, breath came out, but she didn't hear the words.

"I got you, baby," he whispered close to her ear. The heat from his body settled her panic. The hand holding hers played with her fingers, further calming her as a door opened and there was a loud rush of noise before quieting.

"Miss Bennett, glad to see you're awake," a woman said. "Can you open your eyes for me?"

She shook her head no, trying to say, "Too bright." Nox must have heard her as he relayed the words.

"I'll close these blinds," was the reply.

The illumination shadowed by her lids was immediately quenched.

"Is that better?" she asked as Soph gingerly opened first one eyelid then the other.

"Yes." Her voice was getting stronger.

"Mr. Hogan, perhaps you could get Miss Bennett some ice chips from the machine by the nurse's station?" He looked torn at the request. Sophia nodded her head, and he left.

Once Nox was gone from the room, she looked to the nurse, asking, "What happened?"

"You don't remember?" Sophia really had to think about it, but nothing was forthcoming. "You were in a car accident."

Stunned, she took a moment to catalog her pain, associate it with an accident, and it all became clear. Braxton had picked her up, they were going back to Lennox's house. Then, out of nowhere, glass and pain assaulted her entire body. Everything after that was black, unfortunately.

"Braxton?" she croaked.

"Sprained arm, whiplash, bruising. He'll be fine."

Relief swamped her. "And me?"

The cast on her wrist unmistakably stated it was broken. The worst of the pain was in her head and chest, though.

"You have a concussion and stitches in your right leg. Severe whiplash, the broken wrist. Your face was glued back together instead of stitched."

"What!" she cried out. *Glued?*

"Sorry, hon, we didn't think you'd want stitches. It's only a couple of nicks along your jaw and neck." Sophia calmed down, glad her skin hadn't come off or something equally horrifying.

"My chest? It really hurts."

"Probably the seat belt." The nurse leaned forward after checking her IV to show her the marks.

Red, blue, purple, black, she looked like a damn rainbow.

"How long have I been out?" she finally asked.

"You woke up about an hour after you were brought in, but you've been out for about two days. Mostly from the medication we've been giving you."

Made sense.

"When can I leave?" She hated hospitals. There was no reason for her aversion other than they felt as sterile as her home did.

"In the next day or two. We want to keep monitoring your concussion because we haven't been able to wake you as often as we'd have liked to."

Taking it all in was difficult. She didn't remember the crash or waking up before now. She didn't get a chance to dwell on it for too long as Nox walked back in the room with the ice chips. Her mouth watered.

Sitting on the bed beside her, he looked her over as if he hadn't seen her in years. Like something bad had happened in the few minutes he was gone. She had to admit, even if it was only to herself, that she loved the feeling as it washed over her. Having someone care about her well-being, what happened to her, it was a nice change of pace as he slowly fed her a small spoonful of ice. The coolness from the chips revitalized her senses. Her parched throat felt immense relief at being hydrated again. It did remind her of one glaring fact, though. "I'm kind of hungry," she whispered just as her stomach growled with a roar. Embarrassment had her cheeks flaming red.

Nox chuckled, and the nurse smiled, telling them, "If you'd like to get her something, you can, but nothing too heavy. Take it easy for now." She left after that.

Gliding a finger down her uninjured cheek, he asked, "How are you feeling?"

"All things considered, not horrible. I hurt, and I'm terrified, but I don't want to run away." She had a habit of doing that when things got to be too much.

"Do you need something for the pain?"

She gave him a funny look. "The nurse just gave it to me."

He inspected the machines to her left. "Right." He laughed at himself.

They both got quiet after that, lost in their own thoughts. The moment was broken once again by her rumbling stomach.

"Shit," he muttered. "Ma and Loch are on their way, I'll have them get you something." She watched as he pulled his phone from his pocket and sent a quick text.

The minute Nox looked into Soph's gorgeous green eyes relief and love swamped him. It was in that very moment he realized how much he loved her. All consuming, devouring, obsessive love.

Till his dying day, he would do what it took to keep her happy and surrounded by his love. The attraction had been immediate and mutual, but now things were changing. His only worry that she didn't feel the same way, or he was moving too fast.

For once in his life, he felt unsure. He knew he'd have to wait and tell her until she recuperated from her injuries, and if he had his guess right, it'd have to be after the danger passed. Because if there was one thing he knew about her, it was that she would question his motives in relation to him wanting to do the right thing.

She'd passed out again after asking him to get her something to eat. He watched her struggle to get comfortable even with the pain medication in her system. Running his fingers through her light curls that seemed to be unaffected by the accident, she calmed a bit, leaning into his touch. He was glad to bring her some comfort as she rested.

A light knock on her door had his head swiveling and body tensing until he saw his mother and brother, followed by Braxton.

"She's asleep." He warned.

"Oh, we won't stay long." His mother walked over to her bedside.

"Can we talk outside?" Braxton asked him, the look in his eyes spoke of his anger and the news he might have.

"Go, I'll watch her," his mother instructed.

"Thanks, Ma," he said, following Braxton to the hallway, Loch along with them.

"You know who did it?" Loch asked before Nox could. His little brother was pissed.

"We do," Braxton confirmed. "Rebecca was behind the wheel. I've also found some new information I have to look into, check the validity of."

"Like what?" he snapped. Rebecca being behind everything wasn't as shocking as it should have been, given her hatred of Soph, but he hadn't expected there to be more.

"I can't say just yet, but if what I've found is true, then everyone's in for a real shocker." Braxton left before he could comment on the vague revelation.

"What the hell's that supposed to mean?" Loch muttered as the other man disappeared.

"Not a fucking clue."

He didn't have time to dig into Braxton's cryptic words, so all the man had accomplished was pissing him off. Soph needed his attention more than anything else at the moment, so he knew he had to let it go.

Heading back into the room, he watched his mother lovingly brush Soph's hair while she slept, being sure there were no tangles left as she went.

He heard the older woman whispering softly to the younger one, and right then, he couldn't have been happier. Seeing the two ladies he loved most in the world acting as though they'd been friends all their lives, melted his heart. Neither wanted to compete for his attention the way he'd seen some women do.

"You picked good, Nox," Loch said beside him.

"Yeah," he reflected, "I did."

Agony assaulted her body as she fought for consciousness. *It shouldn't be so painful, should it?* The beeping was incessant and made her head pound worse with each noise. Her eyes were still sensitive to the light from the open blinds. Shielding herself from the brightness with a hand over her brow, she immediately saw Nox asleep in one of the god-awful recliners the hospital supplied him with. She couldn't imagine that being at all comfortable for his large frame.

"Lennox," she called quietly, her throat dry. He stirred but didn't wake, so she called him again. "Nox."

His eyes slowly opened as her voice registered to

his tired mind. "Soph?" He still sounded out of it. "You alright?" He was beside her in a flash.

"I'm good." She smiled. Moving over, she patted the empty spot beside her. "Lay with me?"

"I don't want to hurt you." He tried to be chivalrous, but she saw the desire to be close to her in his eyes.

"Please, Nox."

He caved easily, sliding under the blanket with her and wrapping one arm around the top of her pillow. As soon as he'd settle into place, she was moving towards him, needing the comfort of his embrace. Her request being purely selfish.

"Careful, Soph," he grumbled when a breath hissed out of her lungs from repositioning herself too fast.

"I'm fine," she uttered as she settled half on top of him. Her broken wrist laid across his hard stomach, and the stitched leg covered over the top of his.

It took a while, but he finally relaxed under her. His hands began running along any piece of flesh he could reach, soon lulling her into sleep once again.

"Miss Bennett?" A soft voice pulled her from sleep.

The best sleep she'd had in the days since she'd been in the hospital.

"What?" She grouched.

"You get to go home today." The nurse's words had Sophia perked up immediately. "I'm going to unhook all the IV and the monitors. The doctor will be in to speak with you in a few minutes about discharge and aftercare."

Her excitement almost couldn't be contained as the woman got to work. Nox still slept under her, so they attempted to keep quiet. After a few minutes, the nurse placed a hand on her shoulder, whispering, "All set. Might want to wake prince charming here soon, the discharge doctor is a bit...boisterous."

"Thank you," Sophia whispered back. Grateful to finally be going home, showering, and feeling human again.

As her caregiver left, the room was shrouded in quiet and a light darkness. It gave her the first few moments of time to think about her life since the accident happened, and her mother's role in the whole ordeal.

Of everything she'd learned in the past couple of weeks, her mother trying to kill her hurt the most. They may not share blood, maybe not even love, but it made no difference. The woman had raised her, at times, few as they were. She'd mothered Sophia.

After spending her entire life thinking there was something wrong with her, to finally knowing it wasn't her fault was a tad overwhelming. It would take more than a few revelations for the damage to be undone.

She didn't know if she could ever let go of the hurt, doubt, and pain. It was ingrained in everything and everyone involved in her life. She felt like the insults controlled who she was in such a fundamental way.

"Stop thinking so hard, Soph." Nox's words were soft but spot on as he rubbed his face in her neck. Breathing in her scent.

"I can't help it."

"None of this is your fault. You can't hold onto it." His breath met her ear with each word.

"Logically, I know that. Emotionally, though? I feel like the signs were in front of me this whole time. Almost like she was slapping me in the face with it."

"I know, baby." He ran the fingers of one hand soothingly along her arm as she thought things over. She didn't want to be defined by how she was treated or who her real mother was or wasn't. Yet, that's all she had been.

Either the bastard child of her father.

Or the hated child of her mother.

It was a no-win situation.

CHAPTER TWELVE

WHEN YOU LOVE WHAT YOU HAVE,
YOU HAVE EVERYTHING THAT YOU NEED.

IT WASN'T long after the doctor left that Sophia was discharged from the hospital, and they were on their way to Nox's childhood home. He still wasn't sure it was a good idea. He loved his mother, but he worried she was going to get all proper on him and make him either go home or sleep in another room from Soph. Frankly, that just wasn't going to happen.

"You doing okay?" he asked as they neared his mother's house.

Her hand squeezed his. "I'm doing well, Nox." Her smile was slightly loopy from the pain medication she'd been given before they left.

"Once I get you settled in, I'll go grab your prescriptions." She only nodded as she was visibly tired and had no energy for anything else.

Pulling up to the house, he saw Levi standing there, waiting on the front step. As he shut the car off, the younger man walked forward.

"How's she doing?" he asked as Nox exited the vehicle. Circling the hood, he pulled his brother in for a quick hug, happy to note no more bruises on his face.

"She's gonna be good. Ma see those yet?" He nodded to the fading bruises on Levi's chin and eyes.

"Haven't been inside yet," he said sheepishly. "Was hoping the arrival of Soph would distract her."

Embarrassment tinged his cheeks as he admitted to using her.

Shaking his head, Nox opened Sophia's door to help her out. Her stiff movements belied her insistence that she was indeed fine.

"Hey, Levi," she greeted through clenched teeth as they held her arms to keep her steady.

"How you doin', sugar?" Nox was amazed at his brother's entire demeanor change. He went from terrified of their mother to sweet to Soph in a heartbeat.

"Good." She smirked. "She's still going to notice." She pointed to Levi's face.

As she started walking and he saw her cringe, Nox said, "Fuck it," and picked her up in his arms. Cradling her to his chest.

"Caveman!" Levi called behind him.

"Whatever, just grab her shit."

"When did I become the doorman?" he heard mumbled from behind them.

"Thank you," Soph sighed against his chest.

To have that sigh from her, he'd be her caveman all day long.

With his arms wrapped so securely around her, Sophia felt a sense of belonging. Maybe it was the drugs, maybe it was real. But with Lennox cradling her so, with his heartbeat in her ear, it felt like kismet. Nothing could touch her when he was around.

She remained silent as he carried her up the stairs into what she had been told was his childhood room. Smiling as she saw the trophies and posters, she could picture him as a teenage boy. Loud, popular, outgoing—even if he thought he wasn't. He was the boy everyone would have flocked to. The girls would have crushed on him, and the other boys would have wanted to be him.

Watching as he lay her down gently on the bed, his eyes kept darting to the posters of the sexy actresses and singers on the wall. A giggle left her when she saw the pin-up girl laying across a vintage car on the back of his door. His cheeks turned a shade of crimson she never thought she'd see on such a confident man.

The pain meds had her lips a little loose as she shyly told him, "I'd do that for you."

Shock lit up in his eyes just as desire replaced it. "The things I'd do to you," he muttered against her lips as he leaned down to kiss her.

"Tell me," she murmured back as her eyes grew heavy with sleep.

"Later, gorgeous. Rest now." His voice was husky with his want for her.

A heavy blanket was laid over top of her as he sat on the side of the bed, one hand running through her hair, the other rubbing her hip.

His presence made her feel safe enough to sleep. To finally rest in a way her body would be re-energized when she woke.

Things were not going as Lorraine had planned. Well, they were, but they weren't. Sophia and Nox were falling in love and how beautiful it was. Her son was the best man for Sophia's soft shell. He treated her like a princess, and she couldn't be prouder of him. But the danger and hurt, that wasn't something she wanted for any of her children. Most especially the young lady she considered her own long before her son claimed her.

Which was why she'd driven to Anthony Bennett's office downtown. It was time the two of them hashed a few things out. Her own husband, bless his soul, had connections from his Army days that extended to her, and she'd put every one of them to use if she had to.

She knew Lennox was leaving stuff out, not telling her or Sophia. It was time to stop the secrets. He didn't need to protect her.

"Can I help you?" the cute receptionist asked from behind her mahogany desk.

"I'm here to see Mr. Bennett," Lorraine responded stoically.

"Did you have an appointment?" the woman asked her, looking down to her calendar.

"Nope." She wouldn't leave.

"Then I'm sorry, he doesn't have time to see you." Her attitude changed to one of impatience.

"Honey, you go ahead and tell him Lorraine Hogan is here. I'm sure he'll have time for me." Feigning a bored stance, she looked at her watch as if to say, *today.*

The young woman got on the phone, and not two minutes later, the man himself came out to get her.

"Mrs. Hogan, how can I help you?"

She eyed him critically, he looked...tired. Worn down. He was also putting on a front for the receptionist.

"We need to speak in private, please," she suggested.

"Of course." He led her back to his office, which to her surprise wasn't nearly as pompous as she'd expected from the things Sophia had told her about her parents wanting to keep up appearances.

"Your daughter doesn't know you at all, does she?" she said walking past him to one of the over-stuffed chairs by the window looking over the city.

"Why do you say that?" he asked, but she saw the shame on his face. He purposely hid this from her. Not letting her in.

"Because your daughter thinks you're a cold, uncaring man. And since my son tells me you only went to the hospital once while she was there for nearly a week, I have to say I agree with her."

He gazed out the window, eyes full of so much emotion she didn't think anyone else had ever seen him so vulnerable. "I always wanted children. I wanted an entire house full of them." His words were wistful, dream-like. "Rebecca didn't."

"So how did Sophia come about, Anthony? That girl thinks she's worthless." She was so angry at the Bennetts.

A deep sigh left his chest as he answered. "Rebec-

241

ca's complaint wasn't that she didn't want children, it was that she didn't want to ruin her figure. So I found a surrogate. Then we found out Rebecca was sterile. Hope, the surrogate, offered her eggs. I wanted children so badly, and Rebecca put on a front good enough to convince everyone it was what she wanted too."

Lorraine could see he was struggling with his emotions. He wanted to shut down, block that time out of his life, but something happened. She knew it. No child was as hated as Sophia without due cause.

"Anthony, what happened?" she asked again, her voice harder.

"I fell in love with Hope." His words cracked, tears streamed down his face, and she finally got a sense of what was going on.

Walking over to him, she gripped one of his hands in both of hers. "Why didn't you leave Rebecca, then?"

Agony radiated off of him. "Because I loved her, too. By the time I found out how insane she had gone, it was too late. Hope had died, and Sophia was here. I had to put my family together."

CHAPTER THIRTEEN

AND TONIGHT I'LL FALL ASLEEP
WITH YOU IN MY HEART.

Nox and Levi were sitting in the kitchen after he'd gotten Soph settled and asleep. He hated what had happened to her. That he wasn't there to protect her when she needed it most. As she'd nodded off, he made a promise to her that he would be there from now on. He wouldn't let harm come to her again.

"You think she'll pull out of this?" Levi asked, breaking the silence they'd been surrounded in.

Blowing out a deep breath, he told the man, "Yeah. I do."

"She's so vulnerable. Her entire demeanor screams it. How can you be so sure?"

Lennox understood his brother's worry. If he didn't know Soph so well, he'd have the same doubts. "You guys don't see her, the real Sophia. At home, she's got fire. I think she's even surprised herself a time or two." He laughed thinking of a couple days before the accident when she'd tossed a plate after he got her fired up and left her hanging because they had to get to work. "There's no doubt she's shy, man, but that girl is stronger than anyone else knows."

"If you say so." Levi's doubt was still clear.

"You'll see."

The front door opening had him straightening up and Levi cowering a bit, trying to hide the fading bruises on his face as their mother walked into the room.

"Hey, Ma," Nox greeted, kissing her cheek as she walked past him and straight to Levi.

"Hi, baby," she said to him. Her hard gaze zeroed in on his brother's face. "Care to explain?" she asked him.

"And that's my cue." Nox got up to leave when her hand whipped back to grab his arm.

"Not so fast, Lennox." Her voice was pure steel. "Lochlan will be here soon. Sit." She pointed back to his chair. "We're gonna have a little pow-wow."

Well, shit. The last time they'd done that was when his father was sick.

"You sick, Ma?" Worry bled through his voice.

She looked genuinely shocked by his question as she met his gaze. "No. Of course not. Why would you ask that?"

"Last time we had a pow-wow was when Pop was diagnosed," Levi answered.

"No, I promise I'm healthy."

Nox searched her eyes for any kind of deception. As much as she could get on his nerves and be slightly over-bearing, he loved the woman to death and couldn't imagine a world without her in it.

Nodding, he sat down as they waited for Loch to

show up. She puttered around, making sweet tea and sandwiches. A task she only did when something was weighing on her mind.

A knock followed by, "I'm here," announced their baby brother's presence. He came into the kitchen, took in their mother's actions as they sat quietly, and blurted out, "You sick, Ma?"

Her motions stopped as she turned to face them. "For crying out loud, I'm fine. I just had this dance with them." Her hand waved to him and Levi. "Sit," she instructed Loch.

They all remained quiet and vigilant as the woman continued to move about the kitchen. Bringing things to the table, going back to the fridge for more. He knew she had to be upset about more than Sophia and what was happening with that if she were so quiet.

When she did finally sit down across from the three of them, he braced for the worst as she opened her mouth. "I went and seen Sophia's father today." Not what he was expecting. "He's been staying cold and clear of her because of Rebecca. Braxton is looking into Sophia's biological mother and her life before the Bennett's found her."

He was torn between anger at his mother for going there when things were unsteady and pride that she was so set on helping his woman. His mother was a formidable presence, and with his experience, he knew Anthony would have tried to hide things from the woman. She most likely forced the truth from him.

"What did you find out that we don't already know?" Nox asked her.

"Not a lot. I mostly wanted to find out his thoughts about everything that was happening. Why he felt the need to distance himself from his only child. She shouldn't feel like she has no one to love her." When he went to speak, to dissuade that notion, she talked right over him. "No matter that we have a significant other that loves us, Lennox, it's not the same as a parent. Having one who makes you feel like you're nothing and the other reinforcing it by not fighting for you? It weighs on a person. I know Sophia is strong. I know she will get past this, but she needs to understand everything that's happened to make her life the hell it has been."

He nodded, understanding what she meant. He couldn't fathom feeling the way she did. He would help her however he could to move forward, but a huge part of that was going to have to be on her father. Anthony had to be the one to make amends.

"Anthony has a meeting today with the police

detectives that Sophia had already spoken to after the accident. He's going to tell them everything that has been going on. All about Rebecca and what she's been up to, as well. It's time for things to end, and I think he realizes he can't make this go away quietly."

Silence remained after her revelations. He was so happy for his mother and the way she'd handled Soph's father.

"Levi," she finally breathed out softly. Almost like she was afraid the other man would shatter from all the questions in that single word.

"Ma," he countered.

Levi had always been a bit of a different man than he and Loch. He had inner demons held on a tight leash, and Nox worried.

"Do I need to worry about those bruises?" she asked him pointedly.

Their gazes held, almost in a stand-off, before he answered, "No."

"You want to tell me about them?" she asked.

"No."

"Are you ever going to?"

"Yes."

"You're safe?" Levi shrugged. "Be careful," she told him with a frown. He nodded. Her gaze moved to Loch. "Anything you wanna share?"

His youngest brother looked like a deer caught in the headlights—eyes wide and skittish, body frozen, looking for a place to run. "No?" Nox had to fight back his laughter.

"You sure?" she asked him.

"Yes?"

"Your answers are more like questions, Lochlan," she pointed out. He finally remained silent by stuffing half a sandwich in his mouth. "You'll speak about her when you're ready." She nodded in satisfaction. As if she'd known all along there was a woman.

"Her?" Levi asked. "Who, her?"

Loch remained quiet. Nox knew there was a girl. He would be surprised if Loch spoke to her, though. He was one of the shyest people Nox knew. In fact, he wouldn't be surprised if his youngest brother was still a virgin.

"No one," he finally answered Levi with a scowl.

There was a protective gleam in Lochlan's eye that Nox saw, and he understood it so much. Respected the hell out of his brother for being so honorable about the whole thing. He worried that it would eat away at him eventually.

Warmth and healing invaded Sophia's sleep. Forcing her eyes open, she saw the moon high in the sky through the window surrounded by stars. It was one of her favorite things about living so close to the mountains. Even being in the city, nature was still present.

Soft snoring behind her had her slowly turning around to see Lennox sleeping softly. The covers bunched around his hips, one strong muscled arm lay under his head while the other lay across his bare chest.

She watched as he slept. His face soft without worry of who was trying to hurt her. Though she figured the answer was her mother. Sophia hated that he was wrapped up in her drama. She wanted so much to run away, let him be free of the stress that seemed to follow her around, but she was self-ish. She knew that the emotions he made her feel would never be found again in her life.

The tattoo on his arm drew her eye as she traced the moon and star with a light touch. Seeing their family name inside the crescent wasn't shocking. These brothers were as close as could be. A hint of jealousy fired her insides thinking of never having that with anyone herself. All her life she'd wanted a sibling. Someone to share her hopes and dreams with.

"I wish I'd met you sooner," she whispered to Lennox. Knowing he wouldn't hear her words while he slept made her confession easier. "I've always wanted someone else with me, to understand me." She closed her eyes and laid back down on her pillow. "I never wanted my mother's wrath aimed at anyone else, that would be cruel, but to have a kinship with someone who wholeheartedly understood would have been nice."

She paused thinking about what life would have been like if she'd had another person there to be with her through the pain. "I used to think I'd done something wrong to have my parents hate me so much. There was even a point in my life where I wished I was dead. I didn't want to wake up with all that hatred anymore. I only wanted to be loved."

Her eyes popped open wide when she felt a finger trail down her cheek. "You are loved, Soph," Nox whispered leaning over her body gently. Cradling her face in his large palms, he leaned forward, kissing her lightly. "I love you so fucking much it's scary. You consume every thought I have, direct every action I make."

She didn't know what to say. She wanted to say

she loved him too. She did. She felt it wholly in her heart, but would he believe her?

Clearing her throat, she muttered, "I wish I'd known you sooner."

"I heard that." He smiled. His dimple came out to play, making her melt.

"I love that you understand me," she said looking through her lashes. "I'm afraid you're going to be hurt, though, and that terrifies me."

"I'll be fine, baby."

"I'm too greedy to let you go," she confessed.

"That's real good, Soph, 'cause even if you tried, I'd never leave. You're it for me, and there's nothing in this world that could rip me away." She believed him. With everything she'd been taught in life, she knew he was the one thing she would always be able to count on.

Hearing Soph's confession of wishing she were dead instead of being around to take the torment inflicted on her nearly had Nox screaming for the injustice of her life.

Almost as soon as she'd woken, he had too. Suspecting she needed a moment when she didn't immediately try and call his name, coupled with her light touch to his skin, he'd remained silent.

Hearing her confession made him hurt for her. He wished they had known each other sooner, too. He'd have taken her away from that hell hole. She never would have known such hatred so long as he was there to protect her.

With their age difference, though, he suspected he'd have gotten into a lot of shit for it. But she was worth it. She was worth everything he would have suffered had they met before.

"How's your pain?" he asked her, needing to think of anything else. This topic wasn't optimal, but it was all he had at the moment.

"It's okay, I suppose. Mostly just my wrist hurts, but the stitches in my leg itch, too." At that word, she reached to the leg and scratched around the bandage.

"I'll be right back," he told her, getting up and going to the bathroom where he knew there was a cream his mother used to give to him and his brothers when they got into their scrapes and wound up with stitches.

Digging under the sink, he knew he was making noise, and his mother would probably come give him shit any minute, but he didn't care. Finally finding it, he was a little bummed out to find it was nothing special and only Vaseline. He'd have sworn it was something else.

Walking back to his old room, he watched from the door as Soph leaned into the spot he'd vacated. Rubbing her face into his pillow and closing her eyes, her entire body relaxed. It was as though his scent calmed her.

Grabbing his shirt from earlier, he quietly closed the door behind him. "Here we go." His voice low so as not to scare her.

"You were loud," she pointed out.

He shrugged. "It was in the back of the cabinet."

"What is it?" she asked softly.

"Vaseline. I'll rub it around the wound, it'll help with the itch."

Taking her leg out from under the covers and easing back the bandage covering her stitches, he was pissed all over again. Seeing the evidence of her injury, thinking of the things that could have gone wrong, left him with a feeling of helplessness.

Soothing the ointment into her skin, she tensed at first, only to relax upon realizing it wasn't so painful. "That feels wonderful."

Once finished, he fetched the shirt he'd tossed on the end of the bed and gave it to her. "Thought you might be more comfortable in this." He hadn't taken her bra and dress off when they got home, so he figured she might be uncomfortable enough to let him help her change.

She looked down to what she was wearing then back to his shirt. The need to remain modest warred with her want to be comfortable.

Want won out.

"Yes, please." Her cheeks went fire engine red when she realized he was going to have to help her.

"I'll close my eyes if you like," he offered. Even if it would kill him not to see her soft curves.

"Not like you haven't seen me nude before." She laughed lightly.

Helping Soph to her feet, she had to hold her good hand on his shoulder to remain steady while his hands wrapped around to unzip her dress. The snick of the claws was loud in the otherwise quiet room. Their breathing picked up as each inch of skin was revealed. His knuckles brushed her flesh every chance he got.

A shiver wracked her spine when he peeled the fabric back from her body. She moved closer to him as he pushed the straps off her shoulders, baring her creamy skin. Leaning forward, he kissed one shoulder as he dropped the material to the ground.

Her head turned towards his as he went to kiss her neck, their lips meeting in a soft brush. "Lennox." Her breath caught as he sucked her lip into his mouth.

"I can't get enough of you, Sophia," he cooed, loving the sound of her name across his lips.

She mewled against his mouth as he pulled her to him. Their bodies were flush as he ran his hands over every piece of flesh he could reach.

"Lay back, sweetheart," he murmured in her ear. She did as he commanded. Nude, except for her little white lace panties before him. Her light hair spread across the bed like a halo, highlighting her innocence.

No matter what happened with her crazy ass family, this girl owned his heart, and he had every intention of owning hers as well.

Sophia's body vibrated with anticipation as Lennox's eyes roamed her naked flesh, devouring every single inch of her he could with a seductive gaze. With one simple yet scorching look, he made her melt for him.

The heat his gaze emitted as he watched her body ready for his touch made Sophia feel more in those moments than she ever had before. He played her body like a finely tuned instrument, and she loved every second of it.

"Nox?" She questioned when he still hadn't made a move towards her.

Kneeling on the bed at her feet, his large callus-roughened hands landed on her knees. Holding her, squeezing as if he weren't sure she was real or not.

"You're every fantasy I've never had, Sophia." His words were sincere, coming straight from his heart. She didn't need him to tell her, his strategic movements spoke volumes. He was worshipping her every curve with barely a muscle moved.

"I'd like to be," she replied back quietly. Her lashes hid her eyes as she watched his hands slide slowly up her thighs.

His big body leisurely covered hers, his stare locked on her eyes gauging her reaction to his every move. Bracketing his arms around her head, he was basically boxing her in. She should feel trapped, scared. What she felt instead was...cherished. Safe. With Lennox, she knew she never had anything to fear in her combustible world. There was nary a doubt that he would let anything happen to her if he could help it.

"I need you to be mine, Sophia. Every inch of

your curvy little body. Every thought. Every breath. I need everything you are to belong to me."

The intensity of his words, the reverence in his tone, it all spoke to her. "I already am." His gaze widened at her words. "Whatever you want from me, Lennox, it's yours." Placing a hand over her heart, she whispered, "My shattered heart, you healed it." Bringing her fingertips to her temple. "My broken mind, you made me believe." Finally, touching her lips. "You made me feel, Nox."

Both of his hands delved into her hair, cradling her head lovingly as his mouth descended on hers gently. As they met, there was no rush, no hurry to reach some end goal. They savored, enjoyed. Gave to each other what no one had been able to before.

"I'm going to marry you, darlin'." His tongue licked inside her lip when she gasped. "You're going to have my babies." Her eyes flew open with shock. "I'm going to be your everything." Her face lit up.

"I'd like that," she told him. His huge grin was enough to know they were meant for each other. There were very few things in her life that she was sure of, but Lennox was her real deal. The one thing she knew she could count on. His words cemented it.

A creak outside the door alerted them to his mother's possible spying. He didn't scramble away from her, though. He smiled like he'd known she would do it.

"Don't worry, Ma, I ain't about to jump her when she's hurt!" he shouted towards the door. Her jaw dropped to her chest, and he just laughed.

"Lennox," Sophia hissed at him.

"She took longer than I thought she would." He shrugged as if it were no big deal.

With her good hand, she covered her face, completely embarrassed that they could have been caught. "Oh my God." Her voice was barely above a whisper.

He continued to laugh as they heard Lorraine's retreating footsteps and the closing of her door.

"Calm down, Soph," he told her, grabbing her good hand to pull her to her feet. Helping her slip into his shirt, she immediately calmed as his scent surrounded her in a comforting embrace. Cuddling into bed, he held her tight in his arms as exhaustion took hold of her again.

"I can't wait for our forever," she mumbled as her body succumbed to slumber.

CHAPTER FOURTEEN

H.O.P.E
HOLD ON.
PAIN ENDS.

THE RINGING of his cell phone woke Nox from sleep before dawn had broken the sky. Searching behind him for the device, the name flashing across the screen shocked him.

"Hang on," he mumbled into the receiver as he struggled to break free of Sophia's hold around his waist. Clearing the bed without waking her up, he stepped into the hall with a brisk, "What do you want?" to her father. The man made it extremely hard for Nox not to snap on him whenever they spoke.

"We need to meet," the man replied. "Without Sophia."

Shocked, it took him a moment to reply. "I won't hide a meeting with you from her."

"I don't want you to, but we need to discuss something without her around. Sophia is so strong, and just because I was an absent father doesn't mean I haven't recognized her strength. She's also extremely fragile, Mr. Hogan. What I need to discuss with you, it will hurt her. And that is the very last thing I want to do." The man sounded tired and remorseful.

"Fine. I can be at your house in an hour." He hung up before Anthony could respond.

Quietly ducking back into the bedroom, he

grabbed his clothes and snuck back out. He didn't like having to slip in and out. Hide something from her. But by the sounds of it, he would need to figure out how to break whatever it was Anthony had to tell him to her in a way that would have the least impact.

Not that he believed that was possible.

If it was bad, he wasn't even sure he wanted to tell her. Seeing hurt in her gaze from words being delivered by him was not high on his list of things to do.

Writing a quick note for Soph and his mother, he placed it on the counter by the coffee pot, knowing that's the first place his mother went to when she woke up. He was out the door in under five minutes and on his way to his shop to check in, and then to Sophia's childhood home with dread lining his gut.

A peaceful pain filled Sophia's body as she slowly woke up to the sun streaming its warm rays through the window. It was one of her favorite things, feeling the heat relax her tense muscles.

Gingerly raising up from the bed, she knew Nox was gone. Not just from the bedroom, but from the house. He had this commanding presence that couldn't be missed when he was in the same space as her, and it was missing.

Where he was off to was the question.

Going to the washroom and cleaning up, it wasn't long before Lorraine was knocking on the door calling for her. "Sophia?"

"I'm up," she responded, entering the bedroom as the woman walked in.

"Oh, you look so much better!" Nox's mom exclaimed happily. "A good night's rest does wonders for the wounded."

"I do feel better." She gave a warm smile back.

"How about we go for breakfast?" At Lorraine's suggestion, Soph frowned, wondering if it was a good idea.

"Where did Lennox go?" She couldn't bring herself to leave the house without him. It wasn't even about him being protective and not wanting her to go. She truly didn't feel safe without him. The thought was surprising and had her frowning. She couldn't be a wuss. She had to get over her fears, not let them own her.

"He had a meeting early this morning," she explained.

"Did he say when he'd be back?" Sophia didn't

want him coming home and them not being there. He'd freak right out.

"No, but we can leave him a note, and Levi will be with us." That shocked Sophia. He had been pretty tight-lipped and seemed to be avoiding his mother. "He just doesn't know it yet." A devious grin graced the woman's face.

"I'll be right down." Lorraine nodded and left her to dress.

Looking for her small bag, she saw it sitting limply by the closet door. Walking over, she wasn't shocked to see her things hanging with Nox's own clothes. It was silly, but she beamed like she'd won the lottery. Seeing their belongings together made her insanely happy.

Choosing the cherry red dress that matched the color of Nox's car, she quickly struggled into it after more cursing than she would ever admit to. Seeing her cute black ballet flats with the tiny red ribbons on the floor, she grabbed them as well as a small sweater to ward off any chill.

Once ready, she headed downstairs just as the doorbell rang. Descending the staircase as Levi walked in, he smiled at her. She returned the expression and was about to greet him when she got a look at his face.

"Oh, Levi," she sighed, worried about the man. Stitches lined his jaw surrounded by bruising. He grimaced when she was on the last step and reached for his face, turning it so she could get a better look. "What happened?"

So much pain lingered in his eyes as he responded flippantly, "Don't you worry about it, sugar."

"I don't doubt that. I'm worried about the damage your body is suffering." He looked away. "And your mind." Their gazes clashed, his own so much like Lennox's and Lochlan's but filled with more hurt and longing than she feared anyone understood. "I know Nox has said it, but I'll listen, too, Levi. No judgment, I swear." Her words were quiet as his mother walked in the room.

He nodded before greeting the older woman. "Hey, Ma." His entire demeanor changed. He didn't look hurt or lonely. He was happy, at peace. A peace she knew wouldn't last longer than it took for Lorraine to turn away rather than scold him for his newest injury.

Sophia watched as mother and son interacted while avoiding the elephant in the room and behaved like everything was fine.

"Let's go, shall we?" Lorraine said to them both.

266

"Did you leave a note?" Sophia had nearly forgotten.

"Lennox called. He's going to meet us." Relief engulfed her at the news.

Nox hated the prestigious driveway, the tall pillars. Fucking obnoxious door with its creepy gargoyle knocker. He hoped to hell he didn't have to come here too often after he convinced Soph to marry him.

The door had opened before he had his car in park, and Anthony was walking down to him. "Good morning, Mr. Hogan." He sounded a hell of a lot less pained now than on the phone.

"Mr. Bennett." He nodded, walking around the front of the car.

"Thank you for coming. Inside, shall we?"

Nox followed behind the man, wary of whatever was going on and the news he'd wanted to share. As they stepped through Anthony's office doors, two other men were there that he didn't recognize.

"Mr. Hogan, these are Detectives Vichy and Cassidy. They have been investigating Rebecca and my suspicions."

"Mr. Hogan." They greeted him at the same time. He nodded and looked back to Anthony with a raised brow in question.

"Some things have come to light, Mr. Hogan."

"It's Nox, Anthony. I'm marrying your daughter, might as well use my name," he told the man bluntly.

His shock was quickly masked but not before Nox caught a quick glimpse of it. "Right, then, Nox. Evidence has confirmed that it's been Rebecca doing all these things to Sophia."

Detective Cassidy took over. "There was DNA evidence belonging to Rebecca in the car that crashed into Miss Bennett, as well as the threatening notes. We can also put her cell phone in the same vicinity as the phone used to text Sophia. All evidence points to Rebecca working alone."

Satisfied they could put the crazy woman away, he only had one question. "Why?"

Anthony looked saddened. "I always thought she was vindictive and mean to Sophia because I fell in love with the biological mother and that her jealousy was over any attention I gave to our daughter. I really did. What Sophia doesn't know is that her real mother had another daughter. A daughter only two years older." He pauses to look away and clear his throat. "Elianna has been trying to get in touch with Sophia and me for a few months now. Turns out Rebecca has been able to intercept nearly every contact."

That was a bombshell Nox hadn't been expecting.

"So you think this is because of her then?"

"Directly, no," Vichy began to explain. "We believe Rebecca sees her as a threat to her entire life. That she may think Elianna will topple her world."

"Then I don't understand why Sophia is targeted?" He was getting frustrated again.

Anthony's sigh had him looking back at the man. "Because if I didn't want Sophia, Elianna wouldn't be a problem. Rebecca sees Sophia as the problem, her only problem. To Rebecca, eliminating her is reasonable."

His ears rang.

Eliminate.

They couldn't possibly be saying...

The looks on their faces spoke the truth.

"You think she's going to try and kill Sophia." Nox didn't voice it as a question. He knew the answer. "I have to go," he rushed to say, turning for the door.

"Lennox, wait!" Anthony called as he was

halfway to the door. "Rebecca's in custody." His feet stopped. His forward momentum nearly had him face-planting on the floor.

"You have her?" He looked to the detectives as they followed him.

"We do."

"Will she make bail?"

"Even if she does, I won't pay it, and I'll make damn sure no bail bondsman in the state does either," Anthony snarled.

"I thought she had money, too?"

"All the money is mine." A sick smile played on his face.

"I'm going home to Soph. I assume you wanted me here so I could explain this to her?"

"I think she'll take it better coming from you than from me," Anthony said. "I'd like to be there for her, though. Be the father I used to be for her." Nox could tell he meant it. Nodding to the man, he walked out the door, dialing his mom's house as he ran to his car.

She picked up as soon as he'd buckled in. "Hey, sweetheart, how'd things go?" He'd explained in the note who he was meeting just not why.

"Good, Ma. I've got good news for Soph. She up yet?"

"She's getting dressed now. Levi's on his way over, and we're going down to the Waffle Shack for breakfast." Her voice was relieved.

"I'll meet you there." He hung up before she could respond.

The drive back seemed quicker than normal knowing they were finally getting a reprieve from all the drama that had been surrounding them. He could finally have Sophia the way he was meant to.

Completely.

Solely.

She would be his, and nothing would stop them now.

CHAPTER
FIFTEEN

EVEN THE DARKEST NIGHT WILL END.
AND THE SUN WILL RISE.

THEY WERE JUST BEING SEATED at their table as a rumble washed through Sophia like the rain of a stormy night.

Nox.

Her body lit up when she saw his car roll into the parking lot through the huge windows of the restaurant. Needing a minute alone with him, she excused herself and went outside. She knew the exact moment he laid eyes on her. His gaze lit up with excitement and heat as they grazed her body like a whispered caress.

A smirk played on his lips as he looked from her to his car and back. The blush working up her cheeks was from her mind playing back the scene when he first picked her up, and she mentioned she had a matching dress to his car.

His steps as he walked towards her were full of purpose as he reached his destination. One hand wrapped tightly around her waist while bringing her flush to his masculine frame. They were quiet a moment as she absorbed his warmth and strength. Tightening his other arm around her back, he buried his head in her neck and hugged her tightly to him, lifting her off the ground. Her own arms wrapped around his neck to cradle his head to her from behind.

"Soph." He breathed against her, saying her name like a prayer.

"Is everything okay?"

"It is now," he murmured, kissing up her neck and jaw to finally capture her lips in a passionate exchange. She was so lost in him she forgot they were in a parking lot. That's what he did to her when she was around him. Lennox made it so she got lost in him and him alone.

His hands on her back kept her steady against his body with her feet floating off the ground. His erection pressed against her core, and all she wanted to do was go home. To feel his body sliding against hers as they made love.

Pulling back, out of breath, he murmured so only she could hear as others walked by them. "I want to be buried in you, Sophia."

"Can we go?" she whispered back.

Nox looked away from her for a moment to nod towards Levi who was staring out the window she had seen him from before walking her to the passenger side of his car. After buckling her in and striding around the front, they were on their way.

She had assumed they were going back to his mother's house. Not the case as she saw a few minutes later when they pulled into the driveway of his home. The garage door rose slow as molasses—or that's how it felt, at least—while he drove forward to park them in the enclosed space.

No words were said or needed as she watched him climb from the car, his body practically vibrating with restrained lust. For her. It was all for Sophia. He opened her door, offering a hand to help her out.

Once she was standing and the door was shut again, she cuddled in his arms. Pelvis to pelvis, heart to heart, lips to lips. He carried her to the front of the car and placed her on the hood. Pushing her body down with his, he moved each foot to sit on the edge so her knees were upright, and she was wide open for him. Not once did he break their kiss.

Standing up straight, he gazed down at her, her arms splayed out to the side, hair a mess she was sure, and her need for all things Lennox reflected in her stare. His hands roamed freely up and down her chest while he watched her breathing pick up speed. His own nearly matching her. The intensity in his midnight orbs had her lungs stuttering to draw in air. He was a man possessed. The look so feral, powerful, as he gripped his shirt from behind, pulling it over his head and tossing it to the ground.

His muscles rippled with uncontrolled movements. Almost like he would break free of his skin if he didn't have her. She'd never seen him so...aggressive. And yet, as he drew the skirt of her dress up to her waist and removed her panties, his touch was gentle, loving, as his fingers drew lines on the insides of her thighs.

Her eyes closed of their own volition so she could savor every touch, every movement of his strong hands against her cool flesh. The only sound in the room, their combined harsh breathing.

Turning her head to the side as she heard the quiet snick of his zipper lowering, a salacious smile formed on her lips.

When he ran a finger through her arousal, she gasped at the unexpected move. His chuckle made her cheeks warm.

"Just like this, Soph." He groaned as he placed the head of his cock to her willing pussy. No barriers. Just him and her. "Always like this."

She savored the sweet slide of his throbbing member slowly penetrating her channel. Feeling the ridges and veins of his flesh pulse against her inner walls had her back arching and a low moan breaking the quiet spell they were under.

His pelvis was flush to her own when his hands squeezed the insides of her thighs just above where their bodies met and let out a deep growl of satisfaction. "The sweetest fucking burn, baby." His grunts made her giggle, which in turn had her tightening around his length and him cursing, again. "Fuuuck." The word was drawn out and full of desire.

Lennox made her feel worshipped when she was in his arms.

Jesus fuck. Sophia was going to kill him. Her shy looks, tight embrace, and heated eyes had Nox on the edge of control. The way she watched his every move as he slowly began pumping in and out of her sweet, silky depths. A place he never wanted to leave. He would happily stay planted inside of her for life.

Lifting her dress further up her body, he rested it just under her succulent tits. He watched the way she would hold in her breath when he rubbed against her sweet spot. The way her stomach rippled with every exhale when he afforded her a quick second of relief.

On one such inhale, a picture entered his mind clear as day. A small round bump for him to protect and cherish. A life for him to create. A child for them to love.

In a flash, he saw it all: the pregnancy, the birth, Sophia glowing with motherhood and growing into the amazing woman he knew she was. His eyes shot to hers when the image was all he could see. His hands slid up her body to cradle her delicate stomach, thumbs smoothing down the skin to her tight little cunt which was currently trying it's best to suck his seed from the very depths of his soul.

"I can see him, sweetheart," he whispered.

"Who?" She gasps when he buries himself inside of her and doesn't move.

"Our son." His voice steady, her green eyes wide with shock.

"He'll have your eyes." He began pumping his hips again, slow and steady. "My strength." Her hands cover his. "Everything we are will be inside of him." Her eyes glazed over as hips moved faster and the seed was planted in her mind.

He would never force her; the choice had to be hers. But fuck would he love it.

"Oh, Lennox," she cried as her walls tightened and pulsed around his slow-moving cock. Her body tensed with her orgasm. The slapping of flesh against flesh, the only sounds in the garage as they came apart.

Nox's own release was fast and furious as he

followed Sophia over the edge into the abyss. His body tingled with awareness that this could be the time he impregnated her. Their bodies shuddered and vibrated together as they came down from their euphoric high.

Wrapping her legs firmly around his waist, he brought her body flush to his and carried her inside on wobbly legs. Only making it as far as the couch, they crashed down in a heap of limp limbs.

The words, "I saw him, too," followed Nox into blissful slumber.

Sophia laid on top of Nox as he slept, unable to get his words out of her mind. *I saw him.* Their son. A child made of love and harmony. How badly she wanted that. More than her next breath. But it couldn't be, not until her mother was locked away for her crimes against her. She couldn't live under a cloud of grey trying to bring a child into this world knowing someone was trying to hurt her.

She wanted children. Heaven and Earth did she ever, but there were so many other things she wanted to do as well. Meeting Lennox opened so many doors for her. Working in his shop, even as entry-level as being the receptionist, she found she enjoyed the work. The idea of going to school wasn't as out of reach as she always believed it to be.

Lennox made her believe she could do anything.

Something she had to ask herself was, was she ready to give it all up for children?

The answer was complicated.

CHAPTER SIXTEEN

THE GREATEST GIFT OUT PARENTS GAVE US.
WAS EACH OTHER.

STRETCHING, Nox's back cracked and popped from sleeping so awkwardly on the sofa all day. They'd left the Waffle House, made love on his car, and crashed on the couch. It was both the best and worst sleep he'd had in a few days.

Untangling himself from Soph's relaxed body, he quietly crawled off the couch intent on making something for them to eat before she woke up. He also had to tell her about Rebecca being locked up and Elianna trying to find her.

He was more afraid of how she would take the news about having a sister she never knew about. It was a conversation he both dreaded and looked forward to. Foremost, she had to know she was safe.

Pulling out what he needed for fajitas, he got to work defrosting the chicken and chopping the vegetables. By the time everything was cooking and nearly ready to plate, Soph walked into the kitchen looking perfectly ruffled and satisfied. Her hair was a tangled mess, her eyes looked bright with satisfaction, and she was back to her shy self. Hands twisted in front of her and a light pink blush covered the round apples of her cheeks.

"Hey, baby." He greeted her, reaching into the cupboard to grab a glass, filling it with the orange juice she liked. "How'd you sleep?"

"Good," she said, unobtrusively watching him move around the kitchen. "What are you making?" Her eyes closed as she smelled the aromas from the spices covering the chicken he was broiling.

"Fajitas." Tilting the pan with the vegetables to show her, a thought hit him, and he asked, "You don't have more allergies, do you?"

"Just the eggs."

"Good to know." They're silent again as he finished grating cheese and plating the warm tortillas. Putting one plate in front of her at the table, he went back for the chicken in the oven before sitting down across from her.

A few minutes more of quietness while they got their meals ready and Sophia broke the silence. "Is everything okay, Lennox?"

His head shot up at her question, not realizing he'd given away his thoughts. "We need to talk, Soph." He placed his hands on the table, reaching for hers.

"Okay." The simple word was barely audible as fear shone dominantly through her gaze.

Squeezing her hands in his, he smiled reassuringly. "We're alright, baby." She nodded, some of the fear in her eyes alleviating. "Anthony contacted the police about Rebecca." He refused to call the cold-hearted woman her mother ever again. "They've collected enough evidence against her to have her arrested." Sophia paled at his news. "She's in jail, Soph, and Anthony has refused to help her out with bail, lawyers, anything." Tears pooled in her eyes, leaving him confused. "Talk to me, baby." He pleaded.

She withdrew her hands from his, drawing into herself. Her eyes dimmed. He was taken aback when she pushed her chair back and stood from the table as if to leave. Her hands flexed at her sides, her legs twitched as though she wanted to run. He'd never seen her quite so...enraged. It took him a moment to see it, but plain as day, he saw the way she struggled to control the emotions swamping her, fury the prime contender in her eyes as he saw the fire building within.

Walking around the table to her, he wrapped her in his arms, hoping to calm the explosion about to break within her. Cradling her head to his chest, he kissed her temple, asking, "Why the anger?"

Her gaze cleared as she met his eyes. "I don't...I don't know," she responded weakly.

"She won't get away with what she's done." He tried to comfort her.

"I know." Her whispered words were confused. "I want her to pay, but I don't understand my father. Cutting her off? What if she is mentally ill? What if she needs help? The courts will toss her in some hole-in-the-wall psych facility and never think of her again." There was that anger again. "I know she's not the best person, but I wouldn't wish someone to be lost in the system that way."

He understood her anger and confusion then. "Baby," he pushed her away a little bit to be level with her intense pools of green, "you are too fucking caring." Her brows drew together, and when she went to say something, he interrupted her again. "Anyone else wouldn't care about her fate. They'd let her rot. You, however, give a damn. Much as I hate that, we'll help how we can when it's time, alright?"

Sophia mulled over his words before smiling back at him. "Thank you for understanding, Lennox." She leaned up to kiss his chin.

His girl, a true altruist, living amongst a jaded damned world.

He wouldn't change her for a thing.

"There's more, though, Soph." His words penetrated the quiet moment.

"What else?" Sophia asked, straightening her spine. Ready for whatever bombshell he was about to drop.

"The reason Rebecca started all of this..." She watched as he paused. His eyes reluctant to tell her whatever he had to say.

"Please tell me," she whispered. She didn't think she could handle any more surprises but had a feeling this one would be a doozy.

Blowing out a breath, he continued. "There's a woman, her name is Elianna." He paused again, searching her eyes for something, recognition maybe? "She's been trying to get in touch with you and Anthony."

Didn't seem like a big deal to her. "Why?"

"She claims to be your sister." Anything he said after that hadn't been heard. Her ears were ringing. Her breath had stalled in her lungs, and suddenly, her legs turned to jello, and she shook.

"Sister?" she repeated. At least she thought she had.

"Yes," he confirmed.

Sitting back down, she couldn't believe what she was hearing. "I don't even know these people."

Nox knelt in front of her, both hands on her knees. "They kept secrets to protect you, baby. This isn't on you."

She didn't move, didn't respond. How could she? Everything she knew was a lie. Every birthday, no matter how miserable, every function she was forced to go to, it was all a lie. How was she to believe anything anymore?

"Soph?" Nox called to her softly. "Don't shut down on me, baby." She was trying, really she was, but she couldn't help it.

Standing again, she pushed him away. Feeling like a complete jerk, she told him, "I need to be alone," and walked from the room. He called her name, but she couldn't respond. She just needed time to think. To come to grips with everything she'd found out.

Walking out the front door, she was unsurprised when Braxton fell into step beside her. "Go away," she mumbled to him, not bothering to look at him as she walked.

"Not happening," he responded while texting someone. Chancing a look over, she saw Nox's name at the top of the screen. "Don't worry, I told him I've got you."

"Thank you," she whispered.

As much of a pain in the ass as Braxton could be, she knew he'd leave her alone to stew in her thoughts. Nox wanted to fix things. He wanted to conquer the world for her, and she loved that, she honestly did. But this was one thing he couldn't fix. She had to find out on her own what it all meant to her. How to work through her emotions and decide on what to do about her sister.

Sister.

Elianna.

She had a sister. Her entire life she'd wanted a sibling. She had wanted someone to share things with, to make her feel like she wasn't alone in her cold home. Now she had one, and she felt nothing but betrayal.

"Don't close him off," Braxton warned her after a while.

"I'm not," she mumbled, not up for talking.

"You kind of are," he pointed out.

"Go away." She repeated her earlier statement.

Gripping one arm, he pulled her to a stop on a street she didn't even recognize. "Not happening, Sophia. Now listen to me. He's a man. We naturally want to fix things for the girls we fall for. Let him."

"How exactly is he supposed to fix this, Braxton? In a matter of days, I've found out my torturous mother isn't actually my mother, and my father fell in love with my real mother, but she died, so he stayed with a woman who hates us both. Now, I find out I have a sister! A fucking sister. Someone who could have alleviated the pain of being in that house. And God only knows where she's been since our mother died. Do you know, Braxton? Have you met her?" She was yelling, and she couldn't help it.

"You said fuck," he pointed out, and she wanted to kick him.

"That's what you took out of that?" she barked at him.

"What I took out of that is that you're scared as hell. Your entire world is changing, and you don't know how to process it all. Can't say I blame you there, kid, but let me ask you this. Are you more afraid of the revelations with your family, or what Nox makes you feel?" His words were a slap in her face.

"What?" she whispered, perplexed.

"Through all of this, with every secret revealed, you've run to Nox. Now, when there's this, a sister, you're running from him, Soph. That man fucking worships the ground you walk on, and you're running."

The wind got knocked from her as the truth of his words sank in. She was running. She didn't mean to. Subconsciously, the thought of her parents lying to her for so long and so deeply must have had her thinking Nox could, too.

"I didn't realize." She heard how horrified she sounded to her own ears.

"Soph?" Lennox's voice penetrated her fogged mind. Looking around Braxton, he was there, watching, waiting.

Strong.

Solid.

Hers.

"I'm sorry," she whispered, her voice cracking slightly.

He opened his arms for her, and she ran to him. Uncaring of the stitches in her leg pulling or the pain in her wrist throbbing, she swung her arms around his neck.

"I've got you, Sophia."

Did he ever. She never had a doubt about that, but she had doubts about her own worth when it came to loyalty and love. Because if her parents could burn her so deeply, how could someone else not? It was something she would struggle with for a while.

"I need to see her," she murmured in his ear.

"Elianna?" he asked.

"Rebecca."

He pulled away, gauging the seriousness in her eyes. "Are you sure?"

"Yes." Her voice didn't waver. She needed closure.

CHAPTER SEVENTEEN

SOMETIMES YOU DON'T GET CLOSURE.
YOU JUST MOVE ON.

"Miss Bennett, are you sure you want to do this?" Detective Vichy asked Sophia for the third time as they stood outside the interview room at the police station. It had taken nearly a week to get the interview set up because Rebecca had to be processed and charged.

Nox had held her hand through the bail hearing that morning as Rebecca was denied bail, and her lawyer had pled insanity as a defense against all charges. Anthony kept his promise of not helping Rebecca financially until Soph had demanded he do it. Citing that she was going to need more help than the state could ever give her.

Soph's heart was far bigger than any of theirs, and he figured that's why Anthony found a good attorney that understood what Rebecca needed rather than what she wanted. It was a unique situation in regards to the usual attorney-client relationship.

Anthony met with a judge to expedite an order to declare Rebecca mentally incompetent, therefore, giving him all the control of her well-being. He wasn't letting her off the hook, but she wouldn't be treated like the common criminal either.

Nox still wasn't sure how he felt about that.

Personally, he wanted Rebecca to suffer the way she'd made Sophia throughout her entire life.

"I'm sure," she nodded to the detective. As he opened the door, she took a deep breath before straightening her back and walking through. Nox's own gaze remained on her, it was all he cared about. Needing to read her body language so he knew when it was too much for her. When Rebecca said something to strike a blow, he would remove Soph from the room.

At her startled gasp, he looked towards Rebecca and was satisfied that she wasn't having an easy time of it if appearances could be anything to go by. Her hair was greasy and flat. Her cheeks sunken in, and bags of exhaustion lined her eyes. She had a dead look in her gaze that worried him for Sophia's sake. She was a woman who had nothing to lose.

"The praised child makes an appearance," Rebecca cackled as Sophia sat across from her. He stood against the wall beside Detective Vichy, watching the interaction.

"Hello, Rebecca," Soph greeted the woman.

"What do you want?"

"I wanted to see how you were. To get some answers if possible." Sophia's words were clear and strong. He was proud of her.

"You put me here. What do you care how I am?"

"You put yourself here, Rebecca."

The cuffs around her wrists jangled as she moved in her chair. "If it weren't for you, this wouldn't be an issue." Her voice was cruel.

Soph sits tall, ignoring the obvious taunt. "Why did you go through with it if you didn't want me? Why not leave?"

Laughter was her only answer.

"Why, Rebecca?" Soph asked again through gritted teeth.

"Because Anthony had what I needed." The bored tone of her voice said it should be obvious.

"Money," Nox spoke up.

Her eyes shot to him as though she hadn't known he was even in the room. He felt dirty as she looked him over and a sick smile formed. "Well, hello, lover boy. How about we kick these people out and have some fun, you and me?"

"Not a fucking chance. Answer Sophia." He refused to even look at her. She needed to know she was no one to him. Nothing.

Pure rage lit Rebecca's eyes as her legs bounced under the table. Taking a step forward, he knew she was going to lash out.

"You're the only reason he gave me money. I was

to take care of you, and he'd keep me flush. Then when I tried to throw you away, he paid me to stay away from you. The name calling and degradation were just for fun." She laughed when Soph gasped. "You are the dumbest person I have ever met. The drugs I fed you as a child to shut your yappy mouth up are probably to blame for that. But stupid you are, so I win." She sang the last few words in triumph. As if they were true.

Looking down at Soph, her little body vibrated as she stood, her hands balled into fists after pushing her chair in. Walking towards the door, he followed her. She stopped and replied, "If I'm so stupid, why are you the one in cuffs? Why are you the one that's going to spend your life in a mental institution? Don't mistake my kindness for weakness, Rebecca."

"Why's that, you snotty brat?" She was downright belligerent now.

"Because if it weren't for me, you'd be treated like a common criminal instead of a human being."

Her words left their intended mark as Rebecca started screaming obscenities at them when they walked out. The door slammed shut behind them.

"Take me home," she whispered to him, grabbing his hand with a tight grip.

Sophia hadn't known what to expect when she requested the meeting with her mother. The woman looked ill, like a disease was swallowing her whole, and in a way, she supposed it was. She couldn't drink away her pain anymore.

"Why didn't she mention Elianna?" she wondered aloud. She'd asked point blank why Rebecca had done what she did, figuring she'd throw it in her face about having a sister and not knowing her. It would have been a chance for her to hurt Sophia. The thought that Rebecca was trying to protect her from that particular surprise had crossed her mind. But it was unlikely, so she had to wonder about her motivation.

"I don't know, baby." Nox was still holding her hand as they drove.

The following silence drew her in as the movement from the car swayed her into a light slumber. In passing, she wondered why they weren't home already, and when had they left the city? Trusting Nox, she knew he wouldn't steer her wrong with whatever he had planned.

The slamming of a door woke Sophia from her impromptu nap as she watched Nox round the hood of his car. Searching her surroundings, she saw only one other vehicle in the small parking lot of what she recognized as the park he'd taken her to on their first date.

"Hey baby," he murmured opening her door. "How do you feel?" His fingers traced her cheek as he spoke, and she loved the feeling of him touching her.

"Better. Why are we here?" She was beyond puzzled.

"I love you, Sophia, so fucking much. I know you're not ready to say it back, and that's okay." Her head tilted because even though he said it, he also sounded slightly panicked. "I brought you here to meet someone."

"Who?" she asked warily.

"Me," a perky voice said from behind him. Looking over his shoulder, Sophia saw a woman who was the polar opposite of her—tall, skinny, light red hair, tattoos on each arm and along her legs. The one thing she did recognize was the eyes. It was like staring at her own reflection.

Soph's gaze flew to Nox's in surprise. This was her. Her sister. Elianna.

Clearing her throat, she stood, wiping her suddenly clammy hands on her dress before saying, "Hi, I'm– "

"Sophia, I know." The woman glowed. "I'm Elianna. And after seeing your eyes and little upturn of your lip, yeah we're definitely sisters." She smiled, a real, genuine, happy to meet Sophia smile.

"Hi," Soph murmured again. Completely speechless.

"You said that," Elianna laughed.

Looking back at Nox, he was grinning like a fool as tears misted Sophia's eyes. "Thank you," she mouthed to him.

He stepped forward, wrapping one hand around her neck and bringing her in for a kiss, as he growled, "You're welcome," against her mouth. Nipping her bottom lip, he let her go.

"God, you two are disgustingly cute," Elianna told them bluntly, a smirk on her lips.

"I don't know what to do here," Soph admitted.

"Wouldn't expect you to, so let's start with the basics, shall we?" Soph nodded at her question. "I'm the big sister, so you need to listen while I impart this perfect piece of wisdom on you, got it?"

"Uh, yeah, sure," she stuttered, thrown off balance by the other woman's confidence.

"Tell the damn man you love him, too. He's a keeper." She crossed her arms and tapped her foot as if to say get to it, girl.

Turning once again to Nox, the fool had a grin on his face the size of the equator. Pointing to her, he laughed. "I'm going to like her."

"She's right, though," Soph said softly. "I've loved you from the moment I first saw you. The way your back muscles rippled, the way your arms flexed. The rough timber in your voice. Your light blue eyes, clear as the sky, I loved it all. I love you, Lennox Hogan."

He pulled her to him again, picking her up and spinning her around, so she was sitting on the roof of his car this time. Her hands went directly to his hair, playing with the soft, short strands. "I know you do, Soph. Never doubted it for a second." His belief in her consistently left her feeling amazed that she was so lucky to have him in her life.

"Seriously disgusting," Elianna mumbled behind them. Walking closer, she leaned against Nox's car, one finger playing with the hem of Soph's dress. "Tell me something. You really own your own shop?"

"Sure do," he responded.

"Ever hire a woman?"

"Can't say that I have."

"Want to?" Soph got a kick out of their sparring. This was what she was missing all her life.

"Depends," he told her.

"On what?" Elianna's question was skeptical.

"How good you are under the hood."

The expression that lit up her sister's face couldn't be described as anything other than predatory. "The best."

"Come by tomorrow morning, and we'll see about that."

"Seriously?" The woman seemed to be genuinely shocked he would even give her a chance.

"Be there by nine or don't bother showing up at all," he told her firmly.

"Deal!"

"Now, are we done? I'd like to have my woman alone for a while." He didn't even pretend to hide his meaning, which flushed her cheeks fire engine red.

"Riiight," she winked at them. "Lunch tomorrow, Sophie girl?" Her smile was infectious.

"I'd really like that."

"See you guys tomorrow!" She waved, climbing into her little jeep and speeding out of the parking lot.

Watching as her sister cruised away, she told Nox, "I really like her."

"I'm glad, baby," he murmured kissing her thigh, making her giggle when his light beard tickled her skin.

"Now, will you take me home, Nox?" Her voice was husky as she asked him.

He helped her off the top of the car and into her seat before rounding the hood, and they were on the road again. With the windows down and the wind in her hair, Sophia's mind cleared of all the bad in her world.

The betrayals.

The lies.

The hurt.

Replaced by the love she felt for Nox and his affections for her which he gave so freely in return.

Nox watched Soph covertly out of his peripheral vision as he drove. She seemed more at ease with herself than she ordinarily was. He'd been worried when he told her about everything the week before.

Her sister.

Rebecca being arrested.

He had been concerned she wouldn't be able to handle it. That she would break down. He was incredibly glad she proved him wrong. He was proud of her. In the few months they'd been together, she'd grown from this sweet, shy girl into a woman ready to take on the world.

They stopped on the way home for dinner, grabbing burgers and fries from the BBQ place by their house. Everything was quiet for once, and Braxton no longer followed them everywhere they went. Levi had stopped showing up with bruises all over his face, or he was getting better at hiding them. He still couldn't get his little brother to talk, and it was making him crazy.

Taking everything inside, they decided to sit in the living room. He turned the TV on to some funny rom-com that had Soph giggling almost immediately while they ate. If he did one good thing in his life, it would be to keep the magnificent smile on her face till the day they died.

When they were done eating, he cleared everything away and went back to the living room to find her curled up in the spot he'd vacated. Sitting beside her, he pulled her feet into his lap and began rubbing her legs.

He couldn't get over how silky smooth and long they were. For such a short girl, her legs went on for fucking miles. Her moans as he massaged her muscles had him shifting in his seat trying to gain relief from the tightening in his pants.

When her foot grazed his hardening cock as she moved to sit up, he couldn't avoid the groan that passed his lips. Throwing his head back, he closed his eyes as he felt her getting up, hoping to gain some composure. That went out the damn window when she crawled into his lap, her knees flush to his hips. Her sweet little pussy pressed against his now fully erect cock as he throbbed behind the zipper of his jeans. Her heat could be felt through the denim, making him thrust his hips up into her.

"Touch me, Lennox." Her murmured words in his ear had his hands going to her thighs and brushing up to her ass.

His eyes popped open in shock when he discovered she was completely bare. Nothing covered her pretty little pussy under her dress. She was wide open for him. Ripe for the taking.

"Fuck me," he groaned when she began kissing his neck. The onslaught of sensations between her heated core and her kissing his jaw now made him crazed. Hauling her up in his arms, he carried her up to their room, fully intending on taking her fast and hard. Once she was spread out on their bed, it was a whole other story.

Her soft smile and supple body combined with the scent of her arousal had him stripping first his clothes free of his body and then hers.

Her bruises had nearly completely faded, and she moved her arm more freely with the cast on, thankfully. Seeing her luscious body laid out for his devotion, her legs crossed and twisted to the side. Arms above her head, shallow breaths made her chest rise and fall slowly. What sucker punched him, though, was the look in her eyes.

Lust.

Love.

Complete trust that he'd treat her right.

Smoothing his hands up her legs, he slowly pulled her knees apart, spreading her wide before him. No resistance from her whatsoever. He grinned.

He lightly ran his fingers up the insides of her legs, tickling her slightly to wake up her senses. Soon his tongue followed the same path.

"Oh my," she breathed out as his tongue flicked her little nub. "Lennox," her voice was barely above a whisper.

"Sophia," he sighed against her folds, his warm breath making her shiver. Goosebumps popped up on her skin.

"I love the way you touch me," she cried out

when he kissed her lower lips, playing with his tongue. Pushing it into her tight little hole, he softly licked up every dewy drop of her cream that he could.

Pulling back, he gripped her ankles in each hand letting them slide up his forearms to the crook in his elbow as he slid his hands to her ass cheeks. With a firm grip, he lifted the lower half of her body up to his where he lined up his cock for penetration.

"I love the way you taste," he muttered, lowering his head to meet her lips as she rose up to him. Sucking his tongue into her mouth, he knew she tasted her own juices, and he groaned in pleasure. His cock throbbed and begged for him to take her. To make her theirs again.

In one slow move, Sophia felt all his strength, love, and loyalty as he pushed deep into her depths. Owning a piece of her she never knew existed.

Her soul.

It was his. With everything in her, she belonged to him. From now until the end of time.

Lennox was as deep inside of her as he could get as he slowly began moving his hips in small thrusts.

Every withdrawal pushed on her g-spot. Every inward thrust brushed against her overly sensitized clit. Every move had her moaning with more lust and love than she thought she was capable of.

In, out. In, out. In, out.

It never stopped. He took her over the edge time and again, barely giving her enough room to breathe after each orgasm. Never allowing her the chance to pull away from the emotional overload.

"It hurts," she whined at one point. Each brush from the shaft of his hard cock against her petal soft clit made her cry out from the pain which quickly transformed into pleasure.

"Want me to stop?" he asked, out of breath, and she nearly cried when he went to pull away.

"Please don't," she begged like a hussy.

Sweat poured off their bodies, pooling in every little crevice it could find, but he didn't stop. His pace slowed whenever he was close to his own release. She quickly learned that when he picked up the pace again, he had fought it off for a little bit longer.

"Lennox," she cried when she felt a stirring deep in her belly beyond anything she'd felt to date. "Something's happening," she moaned when he thrust deeper than he had before.

"Let go, baby, give it to me," he groaned harshly

in her ear, sucking the lobe between his teeth. "I need everything you have, Sophia."

How she wanted to give it to him. But she didn't know what it was, what was happening. Her clit throbbed, her pussy pulsed as his thrusts slowed yet somehow deepened. Stars lit her mind as it finally exploded, her entire body tensed. Her ears rang as she cried out with the pain pulsing through her system. Then sweet pleasurable elation stole every slice of discomfort from her body, making every touch, every hair, every fiber of her being light up with nothing but euphoria. She was on cloud nine as she heard Nox come with her, his seed splashing her insides with each pulse of his dick. She felt it when he hit her cervix with the head of his cock, and she knew this could be the moment he got her pregnant. This could be the instant they joined as one person and created something so beautiful and sweet nothing would tarnish it.

"I fucking love you, sweet Sophia," Nox growled as he rolled them to the side. Not once did his cock move from inside of her.

With one leg tossed over his hip, she murmured, "I love you more, Lennox," as she buried her head in his chest and fell fast asleep.

CHAPTER EIGHTEEN

THE BEST GIFT IN LIFE IS A SECOND CHANCE.

"Hot damn, who's the babe?" Joey whistled from beside Sophia as she went through the bookings for the day. Knowing he said that about every beautiful girl around, she didn't bother looking up until the bell jingled above the door.

"Sophie girl!" Elianna called, pure joy in her voice.

"Elianna!" She was beyond excited to see the woman, half afraid she might not have come. Rounding the counter, she went to give her sister a hug but paused, unsure of proper protocol for their situation.

A pout formed on her thick red lips when Soph stopped. "Don't stop now, 'lil sis, gimme a hug." She pulled Sophia into her, and an overwhelming feeling of family and love swamped her. Tears formed in her eyes as she closed them to savor the moment.

"Uh, boss man," she heard Mac call from his position beside Joey. "There's tears." He sounded both amused and scared.

"What the hell are you talking about?" Sophia could just picture the scowl on Nox's face as he walked out of his office.

She didn't care, and it didn't seem like Elianna did either since neither made a move to step back from the tight embrace.

She could feel the heat of Nox's body as he walked up on her, she was that in tune with him. His hand ran through her wavy hair as he whispered only loud enough for the girls to hear. "You're scaring the boys, ladies. They don't know what to do with tears from one woman let alone two."

The sisters pulled away laughing at his comment because knowing Mac and Joey as well as she'd gotten to, she knew it to be true.

"Can't handle a woman in tears, you can't handle her in bed, boys." Elianna smirked at them.

Nox chuckled as he told her, "This way." Curious, Sophia followed them.

She had no idea about cars and wondered what interested her sister. Seeing Nox get his hands dirty was a massive turn on, nevertheless.

Soph watched from Nox's bench where he usually sat her as he showed Elianna around the shop and told her what he wanted to be done and how long she had to do it in. The woman just smiled and nodded like she'd been born in a shop. Who knew where she'd grown up, she might have been. Maybe she knew more about cars than all these men put together. Sophia would love to know that.

Nox walked up to her looking amused and

shaking his head. "She's going to run circles around these guys," he said.

"So, she'll be okay?"

"Oh yeah." He bent forward to kiss her like he always did, every chance he got.

The taste and feel of him against any part of her always sent a shiver racing through her body. When his hands gripped her waist, it was no different.

Pulling away, he helped her off the bench. "Come with me." Dutifully following him, she grabbed her purse from Mac as he handed it to her, knowing full well if Nox were dragging her into his office, they might be a while. She was not even embarrassed about it either.

Closing the door behind him, Nox made his way to his desk where he sat and pulled open the bottom drawer. Reaching in for what he was looking for, he straightened back up, utterly stunned at the vision before him.

He'd known when Soph put on the corset top dress that morning he would be in trouble. After making love all night, she'd been more confident in herself and the way she moved as she got ready for their upcoming day.

Now, fuck...now, the laces of the top were pulled open, her gorgeous breasts spilling through the open top, and her rosy nipples were screaming at him for a taste. The cherry on the cake was the bright cherry red lipstick she was applying to her lush lips. A seductive look in her eye.

Sitting back in his chair, he watched as she moved toward him, an extra sway in her hips as she rounded his desk. Her beautiful tits bounced with each step.

"Goddamn, you look fuckable, sweetheart." He groaned, adjusting his hardening dick as her eyes glazed over.

"I'd like that," she whispered, kneeling in front of him. Her hands reached for his zipper, and his breath stopped halfway to his lungs. "But first I'd like a taste." Her words were tentative but held no less impact on his libido.

His hands moved to the arms of his chairs to grip the edges so hard his knuckles turned white. Her fingers stroked his cock as she pulled it free of his pants. He shivered when she ran a nail across the crowned head. Swiping the small drop of pre-cum from the tip, she brought it to her lips, sucking her finger into her mouth and moaning deep in her throat as she swallowed.

Sweet merciful Heaven.

She was a goddess.

His eyes closed as she continued her torturous tease on him. When he felt a warm puff of air just before his cock head was sucked between her lips, his eyes popped open, and he had to force his body to remain still.

She kept sucking him into the cavern of her warm mouth. Her cherry red lips wrapped around his angry looking cock was killing him. Beautiful torture of the best kind. They were a bright contrast to his tanned skin. Her tongue flicked along the pulsing vein on the bottom of his shaft, and his hands shot to her hair, digging into her scalp as he fought to let her keep the control she had.

"Jesus, darlin'," he grumbled, trying to relax back into his chair as she worked her magic.

Her hands were free to roam his body as her mouth and tongue worked him into a frenzy at an alarmingly fast rate. He could feel his balls ready to explode if she didn't let up soon.

"Soph, baby, I'm gonna come soon." He tried to warn her.

She moaned, taking him to the very back of her throat and swallowing around him.

"Ah fuck!" He gave in to the rush of feelings pulsing through him as she continued working him. His spine tingling was the only warning he had as cum shot from his cock and into her willing mouth.

At the first splash to the back of her throat, her gaze flew to his. He knew what she would see on him. Hooded eyes, a smirk, relaxed yet tense. The lust and pleasure she reflected back at him were a pleasant surprise. She'd enjoyed it just as much as he had.

Slowly pulling away from him, she gave one last lick to the tip before cleaning her lips with her tongue and crawling into his lap. Her breasts still on display. His cock still pulled free of his pants, stained with her red lipstick.

With her head on his chest, happy and content, he knew there was no better time to ask his question, even if it was fast. Grabbing the small box from his desk where he'd put it when she kneeled in front of him, he slid the contents free from its slot.

Looking down at his girl, her eyes closed, he slipped the princess-cut solitaire on her left ring finger. She barely stirred when he spoke. "I love you,

Sophia. From now until forever." She finally looked up to him, her face glowing. "Will you marry me?"

Tears immediately overtook her eyes as she sat up, and her hands flew to her mouth. He knew the exact second she felt it. Her entire body froze, and she slowly pulled her hands from her face, turning them over to see better.

Her eyes were wide and fixed on him when she finally looked down to see what he'd slipped on her hand. "Oh my goodness," she cried quietly. He waited. "Yes," she murmured so low he didn't quite hear her. "Yes, yes, yes!" she screamed, throwing her arms around his neck.

He'd never had any doubt.

In his arms was his whole world.

"I love you so much, Lennox," she cried in his ear. "Thank you for picking me."

EPILOGUE
LOVE. LAUGHTER. AND HAPPILY EVER AFTER.

Three Months Later.

SOPHIA SAT STUNNED in the front seat of Lennox's car as he spoke to her father outside. Rebecca had just been sentenced for her crimes. Not just the threats and assault on Sophia, but she was also charged with the murder of Sophia's birth mother.

Unbeknownst to her or her father, the police had been investigating that death as well. Rebecca had been feeding the woman rat poison for days before she gave birth. She was being sent to a maximum security psychiatric facility for the rest of her life.

Sophia figured she should feel relief, but she didn't. She was sad for the older woman. She was sad for her father. She was just at a loss with the whole situation.

It had taken some time, but her life with Nox was finally moving forward. He made it his mission to have her smile and laugh as often as possible. He'd encouraged her to enroll in a few online courses for administration as well. She didn't want some fancy education when she knew that as soon as they were married and started having babies that she would want to stay home with their children. She wanted to be the soccer mom, go to PTA meetings, carpool on Mondays. She wanted the simple life, and Nox did as well.

When she saw him move away from her father,

she smiled at the man who'd raised her, knowing he was finally getting the closure he needed. Nox climbed in the car and told her, "He wants us to come to dinner tonight and bring Ma." He was frowning as he spoke, and she knew that was never a good thing.

"Why?"

"I figure he's going to try and convince us to let him pay for the wedding again and use Ma to do it." Lennox had a hard time saying no to his mother.

She laughed. "You know you're going to lose, right?" As soon as her father had asked if he could help and Nox had said no, she'd known Anthony would use any means necessary to get what he wanted.

Nox sighed as he answered, "I do now. Doesn't mean I have to like it." He grumbled as he drove them to his shop. Elianna was supposed to be back by the time they arrived.

She had to leave a month ago when a close friend of hers had gotten sick. She'd kept in touch with Sophia but not as often as she'd have liked. She was half afraid Elianna wouldn't come back.

"She's coming back," Nox told her. He read her so easily.

323

"I know," she murmured. Her words were not nearly as confident as his.

The rest of the drive was short and quiet. When they rounded the corner of the street that Nox's shop was on, a huge grin appeared on Sophia's face when she saw the mudded-up jeep in the parking lot.

"Told you," Nox quipped as he parked.

Jumping from the car, she ignored him as she ran for her sister. Rounding her jeep, she saw Elianna and Asher in a standoff with him looking ready to strangle the much smaller woman.

"Umm, hi." Her voice squeaked. She jumped when they both whipped around to face her just as Nox appeared behind her.

Asher pointed at Elianna and said to Nox, "Control her, she damn near ran me over again."

"If I wanted to run you over, I wouldn't have missed!" Elianna smirked.

"Seriously, you two?" Nox groaned. "We're starting so soon?"

From the moment they met, they'd fought like cats and dogs. Soph swore it was attraction. They grumbled and snapped anytime she suggested it. Nox generally just shook his head at their antics.

Asher growled at Elianna when she stuck her tongue out at him, and he walked away.

"You gonna stop trying to run over my best employee anytime soon?" Nox asked once Asher was out of earshot.

"Don't you mean second best?" she smart-mouthed back.

"Christ." He grabbed the bridge of his nose and shook his head. Obviously done with the entire thing, he left them alone to go inside.

"How did it go today?" Elianna asked her. Her usually boisterous attitude was gone, and in its place, was the scared little girl she had been all her life.

"She'll never see the light of day again, Eli," Soph told her. Their eyes met with a mutual struggle over whether to be relieved or upset.

Pulling Soph in for a hug, she cried. "Thank you, Sophie girl. For going, for being strong enough to watch and stand up to her."

This, this was the closeness Sophia had been searching for all her life.

Nox watched Sophia all day, expecting sadness to creep in over her mother, but when not a single tear was shed, he felt relieved. The older woman didn't deserve a single moment of Sophia's guilt. He was both surprised and elated when she'd told him she was really alright with the sentencing and Rebecca's subsequent outburst cursing Soph and Anthony to hell and back.

When Anthony had stopped him in the parking lot of the courthouse before they'd left, he'd been pissed, only wanting to comfort Soph. Which is how they'd been looped into sitting at the fancy table they were currently at in the mansion's informal dining room.

Informal his ass.

It was fancier than his mother's Thanksgiving best, and she went all out for every holiday. Without the servants, of course.

"So, Anthony, what was so pressing we all had to be here," his mother asked, never one to beat around the bush.

The older man sputtered at her direct question. "Well." He cleared his throat while wiping his mouth with a napkin. "I'd like for the kids to allow me to pay for their wedding. They refuse."

His mother rolled her hand as if to say "continue".

Anthony darted a quick look at Sophia who just smiled. "They won't accept my offer," he said.

"So I'm here because why?" Lorraine asked again.

"To convince them." He threw his hands up in the air, and Sophia lost her battle not to laugh. "You hush, child," he scolded her.

His mother was completely serious when she said, "Do you think my son can't provide for our girl? That he can't give her what she wants?"

Sophia's laughter stopped, and she shot a worried look at Nox. "I know you don't think that, baby," he whispered to her. She leaned up to kiss his cheek lingeringly.

"What! No. Not at all. I happen to know he's very well off." They all raised a brow at that remark. "Oh, I had to check." He defended himself. "It's a gift. I want to give this to them."

"Oh, Daddy," Sophia beamed at him.

"If you want to give them a gift, give them a honeymoon, Anthony. Send them to their dream destination," Lorraine told the man with a gentle grin.

Looking to Anthony, Nox said, "I'd be okay with that."

He pondered the idea before answering. "Alright. When Sophia was a little girl, she'd always wanted to go to Africa. She was fascinated with their culture."

"I remember that!" Soph spoke excitedly.

"A safari?" Nox asked her.

"Yes!"

"Safari it is," he said to Anthony.

The smile lighting her face, the happiness shining in her eyes, was all his heart could ever ask for.

The End.

Thank you for reading One Chance. The next book in the series is <u>One Choice</u> . You can find a complete list of my books, along with series lists and reading orders on my <u>website</u>.

Please consider signing up for <u>KL's Confessions</u> for a free story as well as first chance at cover reveals, releases, contests and more.

ACKNOWLEDGMENTS

I honestly feel like I could never thank everyone in my life enough.

Kaci thank you for sticking with me. For being my voice of reason and calling me on the things I miss.

Codie thank you for being in my life. I can't picture not ever knowing you.

Katherine mercy, I don't know what I would do without you hounding me every time we spoke.

Bloggers, readers, authors, friends, everyone, thank you for your continued support!

ABOUT THE AUTHOR

Hey, I'm Krystal. I write as USA Today Bestselling Author KL Donn. I'm stoked you've grabbed one of my books and I really hope you enjoyed the story!

A little about me:

Perpetual romantic.

Coffee addict.

I speak sarcasm more often than not.

Gimme an action flick over a romance. But a romance book over action. I'm weird like that.

Did I mention coffee addict?

Closet shopaholic.

Beach lover.

Coffee addict, it bears repeating. Again.

Husband obsessed. Mine that is, you can keep yours.

Mom of 6, well 7 if you count the husband. Oh and 2 of those are a cat & dog.

I love to connect with my readers so feel free to find me on any and all social media platforms you use! I can't promise to be sane, or not swear a lot, but I'll be extra happy to hear from you!

KL's Deviant Readers | Facebook | Instagram | Twitter | Eden Books

Or follow my releases on:

BookBub | Goodreads | Newsletter | AllAuthor

Coming on September 22, 2020 is the first book in an all new series. Possessive Neighbor is the first in the Neighbor Novels.

London's Calling is a sexy standalone novella about a hot brit cop and his lovely Canadian tourist. Coming June 4, 2020.

<u>Imprisoned:</u> A Dark Sleeping Beauty retelling

Task Force 779

Missing in Action | Explosive Encounter | Nowhere To Run

Vashchenko Family

Command

Uncontrolled Heroes

A Girl Worth Fighting For

Daniels Family

Until Arsen | With Kol | Embers Falling

Those Malcolm Boys

Obsessive Addiction | Accidental Obsession

Adair Empire

King | Luther | Castiel | Atticus | Carver | Grasping For Air

Timeless Love

Once Upon A Time | Happily Ever After

In His Arms Series

Safe, In His Arms | Bullied, In His Arms

Naughty Tales

Dirty | Treat Me | Snowed In

The Protectors Series

Keeley's Fight | Emily's Protectors | Kennedy's Redemption

The Possessed Series

Owned by Dominic | One Dance For Case | Lost & Found | Lucky Christmas

The Hogan Brother's

One Chance | One Choice | Unchained

Love Letters

Dear Killian | Dear Gage | Dear Maverick | Dear Desmond | Dear Lena

Stand Alone Books

Brantley's Way | Mr. & Mrs.

Made in the USA
Middletown, DE
08 July 2022

68825679R00192